LIFE INTERRUPTED

DANIELE LANZAROTTA

LIFE INTERRUPTED

Written by
Daniele Lanzarotta

Song Lyrics by Krys Janae

Edited by Amanda Sorrells-Larsen
Developmental Editing by Jennifer Milius
Cover Design by Krys Janae

ISBN (Paperback): 979-8-5000-1582-2
ISBN (Hardcover): 978-1-0878-7892-8

DEDICATION

Okay, this is going to be another unusual dedication...

To my tribe – Amanda, Jennifer, Tara, Krys, and Diksha – thank you for putting up with all the last-minute stuff. I'd love to tell you that things will change, but we all know that isn't true. Lol

To Joc, for finding the perfect voices for Levi and Riley.

And to the characters from the Sinners Series, for creating such a dark place that I needed to create Levi and Riley to balance things out. :D

1

LEVI

THE OPENING BAND is about halfway done when I put on a flannel shirt, a baseball cap, sunglasses, and head over to the floor. The security team hates this part of the show with a passion, and yes, they'll follow me from a distance and monitor my every move, but it is all worth it. We're in Italy tonight and I don't speak a word of Italian. But right now, it doesn't matter. I always thought it was cool how you can sing the lyrics to a full song without actually knowing the language and somehow, feel what the song is all about. But the best part of being in the middle of a large crowd like this is the level of energy. You can't find it anywhere else. People are just happy. And no matter what kind of day I'm having, this right here is what gets me in the right frame of mind for the show. Happy and energized. Of course, there is also the thrill of knowing that someone could recognize me at any moment.

I cheer along with the crowd when the song is over, sweat already dripping off me even though it's cold out. A few more songs come and go, and the opening band asks the crowd in English, and then in Italian, if they're excited for Oblivion tonight. The crowd starts shouting 'Oblivion' over and over again, knowing all too well, we don't go live quite yet. Yep, Oblivion. That's us - me, Bentley, Max, and Kev.

I can't keep the grin from spreading on my face.

I fucking love what I do. I could do it every day, every night… the tours, the fans, the music. I can hardly believe this is my life sometimes.

"Five minutes," Xavier, the head of security yells into my earpiece. All because my pain in the ass manager wants me to have a cool down period before I take the stage.

I look over to where Xavier is and roll my eyes at him. He just shakes his head. We both know this is where I'll be until I absolutely have to go. Especially tonight.

Tonight is bittersweet. Rome is our last show of this tour. Then we're all taking a forced break. And I have no fucking clue what I'm going to do for months, other than avoid going home like the plague.

I look to my left and notice it's not as crowded. There're three women with bodyguards – trying their best to shield them while making a little extra room for them to enjoy the show. The fact they're standing still, looking grumpy as hell as other people jump, dance, and bump into them, is amusing. I look over at Xavier and nod my head toward them.

"The one wearing that stupid shirt with your face plastered on it is some politician's daughter visiting from Japan," he says, and I grin as I look at her. Cute. She looks to be in her thirties. Older. But definitely legal. "Don't even think about it, Levi. If I get one more call from your mom asking what the hell you are doing, I'm going to lose my mind. Actually, forget that. I'm going to tie you to a chair and put the phone on speaker so *you have* to listen to her."

I let out a chuckle.

"Quit grinning like a fool before you get recognized. You know your fans can spot those 'adorable dimples' anywhere," Xavier says in a mocking tone. "Also, time to go back."

That only makes me grin even more.

When I turn to leave, those same women giggle and chat amongst themselves as they keep looking in my direction. I lied before. That wasn't the part that the security team really hated with a passion. This is.

I make my way over to the three women, all while thinking about how I can't wait to ditch this shirt. One of their bodyguards tries to block me and he gets the ultimate glare from the politician's daughter. He steps aside, and I move in closer, putting my arm around one of them – the shy one who is not wearing designer clothes and is blushing. Chances are, she lives in her friends' shadows, and by the glare the politician's daughter is now directing at me, that is about right. But not tonight. I lean in toward her and yell over the music. "Come with me," I start to lead them out as I nod to the other two to follow, hoping they don't do anything crazy until we're out of here and backstage, or Xavier will be cranky as fuck for the rest of the night.

The moment we get to Xavier, he rushes us out of there and toward the back. "You ladies," he says, "Follow Anthony here." He points toward the other security guy. At least, I think he's security. He's new and shorter than I am, and looks like a kid next to Xavier.

"But-" the politician's daughter starts to say, in English, and I stop her. "Go ahead. I'll meet you ladies after the show."

She hesitates. A reaction I've seen far too often. She crosses her arms over her chest and stares me down. She has this look of, "How dare you?" and "Do you know who I am?" Well, security will have fun with this one.

That is when I notice the guy with a scowl next to her, saying – well, yelling things in Japanese. I know he's not security because he's wearing a shirt of our band with a – I tilt my head to the side, taking a closer look at it and I chuckle. Yep. There is a red cross On. My. Face.

Ignoring the guy, I look at the woman. "I promise. I'll meet you after," I say, taking the sunglasses and hat off then and giving her my best smile, and they agree to follow Anthony out.

"Anthony, get rid of the guy," I yell over my shoulders as I jog backstage, taking the shirt off on my way to change out of these clothes and get ready for the show.

RILEY

"Alright, Ladies," Mrs. O'Connor starts to say and the other five dancers are already halfway through putting on yoga pants or changing their shoes to get out of here. "Auditions are in one week. We're taking an hour for lunch, then back to the studio."

I stand here, leaning against the barre as I watch her. She seems off today. More so than she has recently. The one-hour lunch alone is a sign that something is wrong. We usually sit down to eat something quick right in the studio before we get right back to it.

"Are you coming, Riley?" Krissy asks.

I stay. I always do. It should be no surprise, but Krissy still tries.

"Nah. I have to call my mom here in a bit," I say, leaving out the part where I'll use the rest of my time to practice because I need every minute I can get.

"Okay," says Krissy. "But I'm bringing you something to eat."

Krissy is my bff from back home. She's the opposite of me in every single way. From looks, with her black hair and blue highlights, to her outgoing personality. Her parents moved to the U.S. from Korea right before she was born, and being a traditional, reserved family, they often joke around saying that Krissy and I must have been switched at birth.

I smile at her. "Thank you."

We look over to where Mrs. O'Connor is standing, glaring at her phone, and I get this bad gut feeling. Krissy and I are staying with her for the summer while we take her classes before our audition to my dream school. I've taken her classes every summer for the past 4 years, but I've really never quite seen her like this. I know she had kids when she was older because of her dance career. Still, she is in her early sixties and always looked much younger. Until recently. This year alone, she looks like she aged ten years with all the drama from her son.

"Levi has a show in Italy tonight," Krissy says, throwing her dance shoes in the bag before putting on her black vans. "She's probably refreshing his social media every few seconds to see what tonight's drama will be."

I chuckle. "You seem to know a lot."

"Well, one should be well informed, and I'm hungry, so I'm out," she curtsies before she twirls her way out of the room.

My phone rings and I answer right away, seeing mom and aunt Lilly on the screen.

"Hey!" I say cheerfully, trying to hide the fact that I notice how much more weight Aunt Lilly lost. I walk by the window and sit on the floor in a spot that is brighter from the sun. I lean back against the window and stretch out my legs, missing not being back in South Carolina.

"How's the trip?" I ask. "I like the new hat," I tell my aunt, chuckling at her baseball cap with the print, 'Just a Girl Who Loves Beer'.

She smiles. "The trip is wonderful. We're in Greece now. Only one more place to knock off my bucket list, kid."

"Thailand?" I ask.

"Yep. Saving the best for last. We head that way in a few hours," she says with a smile that is the complete opposite of mom's expression.

"What's wrong?" I ask, looking at my mom.

She sighs and Aunt Lilly answers, shaking her head. "Nothing. She just thinks once I complete the list I'll give up. As if," she says. "I need to see my favorite niece get into college and dance her way around the world," she grins.

I laugh. "I'm your only niece, Aunt Lilly."

"And favorite," she says with a smile and a twinkle in her eye that always seems to be there when she tells me that.

I'm completely distracted by her stories of Greece when Krissy plops down next to me with a box of takeout food.

She pokes her head on the screen. "Hi Mom! Hi Lilly," she says cheerfully.

They chat for a bit as I open the boxed salad, and then, we say our goodbyes.

Krissy nudges my shoulder. "Are you going to eat, or just make sure that salad dressing is covering every inch of your food?" she asks as I move the fork around. I don't answer and she knows I'm worried.

"She still doesn't know, does she?" Krissy asks.

Having Aunt Lilly around always felt more like having a big sister than an aunt. She's only seven years older than me. She was nearly done with grad school when they found the tumor. A few months ago, when we found out that Aunt Lilly only has months to live, I told mom I got a scholarship for any school I want to go to, and that she should use my college money to take Aunt Lilly away on her dream trip. She's talked about Thailand since I can remember. She always said she felt like she was born in the wrong place – that Thailand was her home – she could feel it.

"No," I tell Krissy, and I choke up a little. "And I hate lying to them about it, but it was the right thing to do. I'll just have to get that scholarship."

2

ONE DAY LATER - (DAY 1)

RILEY

TWENTY MINUTES. That is all I need every day to keep myself sane. Not much to ask for, right? Twenty minutes to myself. Just me and the music.

Apparently, today isn't going to be one of those days.

I get to the dance studio early, as usual. I put my blonde hair up in a perfect bun, change from my flats to my favorite worn out pink pointe shoes, start my playlist, and roll my neck from side to side before walking to the center of the room. I close my eyes and take a deep breath, but before I can open them again, I hear the giggling and chattering from the other dancers. Melody, the one who loves gossip and drama, is holding up a magazine, while the others try to get a glimpse of whatever she is looking at.

It doesn't take much for me to lose focus. When I'm dancing, I have to be in my own little world. The only sound that belongs in that world is music. Irritated, I sigh as I stop the music. The girls carry on as if I'm not even here. I walk over to my bag, sit on the floor with my back against the mirror, and just scroll through my phone as I wait for Mrs. Connor to get here.

"Come on, that is hot," Viviana says as she stands next to Melody and points to the magazine. I peek over then, and I can see just the top of the front cover – tabloids, of course, and I can take a pretty good guess on who they are talking about.

I roll my eyes and Krissy catches me. Krissy twirls her way toward me. "What?" she asks playfully as she sits next to me. "It's not every day you get to say you know the guy all over these tabloids."

I chuckle. "You don't know him. You know of him." I correct her as I look at the time, counting down the seconds until Mrs. O'Connor is here to put an end to this.

But time goes by, and she is late. I'm not surprised. She was on the phone for at least an hour before we left the apartment.

'What did he do now?' I think to myself.

My phone vibrates and it's a text from Mrs. O'Connor.

Mrs. O Connor: I have to cancel class today. Can you send everyone home? You're welcome to stay at the studio and practice.

"**Got it**," I text her back, eager to have the studio to myself for an hour.

I stand up and clear my throat. When they all stop gossiping and look at me, I say, "Class is cancelled. I'm sure you have your guess on the reason."

Everyone except for Krissy, rushes out of here. Krissy stays.

"Are you staying?" She asks me.

"Yeah. Are you?"

"If you don't mind," she says as she walks to the middle of the room and stares at her reflection in the mirror. She lets her hair down and shakes her head so the blue strands stand out more.

"So, what did he do now?" I ask as I turn on the music, selecting my favorite classical song before I walk toward her. Not caring either way, but more curious about how much of Mrs. O'Connor's time it will cost us.

"According to that magazine, he got arrested."

My eyes widen. Sure, he's reckless, but things never went this far.

"Isn't he overseas?" I ask, curiously.

"Yeah," Krissy says, leaning down to stretch.

"Oh. Arrested for what?"

Still leaning down, she says, "Assault. According to that magazine, anyway, he beat up some guy backstage and there may have been a knife involved."

"Ugh. I guess there goes Mrs. O'Connor's time for the rest of the summer. Baby-sitting a twenty-two-year-old who should know better," I say in frustration.

"Right. Assuming they let him go." Krissy pauses, then shrugs. "Well, don't overthink it. There's not much she can do from here."

"Besides worrying 24-7," I retort.

Krissy puts her hands on her hips as she stares at me. "You got this either way, Riley. As long as we can use the studio, we can keep working on our own if we have to. We got this," she says with a smile.

Just then, I hear the phone vibrate against the floor, annoyingly interrupting the music. Krissy follows me to grab it. Another message from Mrs. O'Connor comes in. I have to do a double take as Krissy reads the message over my shoulder. We look at one another, then check the local news.

LEVI

It's been over 12 freaking hours. I'm still wearing the sweat drenched clothes from last night's concert. My stomach is growling, and the smell of alcohol that was flung on my shirt during the small after party backstage is making me feel sick.

"Levi Jameson O'Connor," a man calls out as he approaches the holding cell. I stand up right away, ready to get the hell out of here.

The police officer who looks way past retirement age, unlocks the cell door, and says something in Italian. Let's just say that the language of love doesn't sound so loving right now. Wait. Was that supposed to be Italian? Or French? It would make sense that French is the language of love. Or was it Latin? Shit. I can't remember. And I have no clue what he said, but I put my head down and follow him out as he escorts me to one of the rooms, where I see none other than my manager, Grant Sullivan, wearing a suit and more hair products than well… more than anyone I know, and that includes that one Jersey Shore dude I've seen on TV.

The man says something else and puts both hands up.

I just look at Sullivan, confused as fuck.

"We got 10 minutes," Sullivan tells me before he says something to the man, who leaves, closing the door behind him.

"What are you doing here?" I ask as I sit down across from him. "I called you to get me a lawyer, and that was last night, in case you lost track of time."

"Well," he says. "First things first, that was at 3 in the morning. And I guess a night in jail didn't help you calm down like I thought it would."

I glare at him. The only reason the band doesn't get rid of him is because he is Bentley's – our drummer's, older brother. And yeah, okay, maybe he knows a thing or two about the business and he brings in the money, so the label loves him.

"Relax. He's working on getting you out of here, or at least transferred to New York," he says in his usual carefree tone.

I'm usually a laid-back person. But when he is around, things change. He has always had this effect on me, since Bentley and I met and became friends in middle school. Sullivan hates my guts too. That's no secret.

I slam my hand on the table, staring at him. "I'm in jail." I pause. "In another country, where I don't even speak the language. I think relaxing is out of the question," I snap.

He still looks unphased. If anything, me being here is making him more money.

"Did you get a hold of the girl? She could testify."

He leans back against the wall, then realizes where he is, moves forward and brushes that side of his suit with his hand. "Yes, and no, she will not."

"I will talk to–"

"No. You will not." He cuts me off. "The headlines are already driving ticket sales up for the next tour we announced this morning. You're accepting the charges. No contest."

"The hell I am."

"Just suck it up and take one for the team, okay? It's a first-time charge. They will let you go with a slap on the wrist."

I launch toward him. He practically jumps back, but he isn't quick enough. I grab a hold of his shirt and twist it in my grip, pulling him forward. "Take one for the team?" I say in between gritted teeth. "I think it's safe to say I've been listening to your bad judgement for far too long," I growl. "What makes you think they'll just let me go after they account for the news articles over this past tour?"

He looks down at my hands and then back up to hold my glare. "I won't think twice about adding a second assault charge right now, kid," he whispers in a menacing tone. "Just sit back and do as you are told. We'll get you home and still benefit from the headlines. It's a win-win."

Suddenly, the police officer barges in, holding a piece of cloth over his mouth and nose and throwing two of the same toward us as he yells at Sullivan and me both.

3

RILEY

Krissy and I can't really focus on anything after reading the news that we're going into lockdown. My stress level goes through the roof and I take deep breaths the moment I feel my heart start racing. That helps, but it doesn't stop the thoughts rushing through my mind when I think about what could happen to our auditions. I feel the palpitations surging when Krissy asks if I'm ready to go.

"No," I tell her, feeling uneasy at the thought of having to walk three blocks in a city that is packed with people coming and going all day. Every day.

Krissy walks up to the windows and looks down. "I think we'll be okay," she says. "It's not that busy out right now."

When we step outside, the streets are much emptier than what I became accustomed to since we came to Manhattan for the first time a few years ago. Traffic is the usual amount, especially now with people going home. But still, it feels like we're living in a different world. People are keeping their distance as much as possible and many are wearing masks or bandannas covering their mouths and noses. We end up stopping at a CVS store in the corner and buying two masks.

We get to Mrs. O'Connor's apartment building and things are already insanely different. The staff are wearing masks, the cleaning crew seems busier than usual. We go straight to the penthouse and take the masks off as soon as we step inside. We're about to turn the TV on, when Mrs. O'Connor comes in. She looks and sounds calm considering what's going on. If anything, she sounds annoyed. "Hey, girls," she says as she puts her keys and sunglasses down on the table by the door. She sighs. "I need you to move to Levi's room. I'm going to drive to Atlanta to pick-up Carly from school tomorrow. I don't want her traveling with all this going on, but it's just an overnight trip. I'll make sure food and everything else is stocked."

"Sure," I say. "Is there anything we can do?"

She shakes head. "No. Just stay in. That's all we can do for now."

Mrs. O'Connor' disappears into her room to pack, and next to me, Krissy can barely contain herself.

Krissy squeals when I open the door to Levi's room. "How lucky are we to be sleeping in his room! On his bed!"

I roll my eyes at her, and I step in first. The dark

blue walls, the black king size... No TV... hmmm, but there is a record player and a CD player near the bookshelves.

Krissy goes on, excitedly. "And the pictures I can post on Instagram of his room. Imagine what that will do! Do you think I can go viral?"

"I'm pretty sure that falls under invasion of privacy," I tell her as I walk in.

She scoffs. "Have you seen the tabloids? Privacy went out the window a long time ago."

She stops when she walks all the way in, and finally seems to calm down. I look at her to see why she is so quiet.

"What?" I ask her.

"Well, this is disappointing," she says as she flops down on the king size bed.

"What exactly were you expecting?" I ask.

"I don't know," she pauses and looks around, then sighs. "Drugs! Blowup dolls! He's a rockstar for God's sake."

"Oh my God, Krissy," I burst into laughter. "At his mom's house? Besides, he hasn't lived here in what? 3? 4 years?"

"Well, I still didn't expect bare walls and bookshelves full of actual books."

"Those are mostly comic books," I point out.

"Details," she rolls her eyes. "And why does his room smell like cinnamon?" She asks.

I shake my head at her. "Again. His mom's house."

"Right," she says. "I bet his place smells of cologne, sweat, and sex."

I glare at her. "Krissy." I say in a warning tone. "Get it together," I laugh.

"Well, I don't care. I'm still totally going to brag about sleeping in Levi O'Connor's bed," she huffs.

"Of course you are," I mumble under my breath as I look at the shelves full of books, in addition to the comic books, and classical CDs, and wonder how someone could change so much.

LEVI

I'm both impressed and disturbed that my mom got involved, and along with the lawyer, arranged for them to let me go. Well… sort of. I'm sure this whole lockdown thing played out to my advantage. The lawyer was able to negotiate admission of guilt with house arrest for 90 days. Mom insisted her home be it, which blows. The lawyer told me they were actually about to drop the charges when mom stuck her nose in my business. No one contested, which really pisses me off.

I have no doubts that lots of strings were pulled. Including extradition to the US, which I'm sure involved the US Embassy, I'm shocked that things moved so fast, and even more shocked that they approved me going back with the guys. Of course, there was someone waiting for me at the airport, ready to escort me home with my brand-new ankle accessory.

Now, here I am, at midnight, standing in front of mom's apartment door, facing some serious lack of sleep. I don't think she's even expecting me until a few days from now, so all I can do is hope she'll leave the lectures at least until after I get some sleep.

Marcia, our housekeeper, opens the door, and I feel the tension leave my shoulders.

She shakes her head before she pulls me into a hug.

"Mr. Levi. You, sir, are trouble."

I pull away.

"But you still love me," I smile.

She shakes her head again as she closes the door behind me.

Marcia is in her fifties. She has been working for my family since I was twelve, and over the years, she became a second mom.

"How mad is she?" I ask as I put my suitcase, a duffel bag, and my guitar by the door. Marcia follows my movement and notices my new accessory.

"Mr. Levi. When are you going to settle down?" she asks.

"Come on, Marcia," I say as I walk toward the kitchen. "You know the real me. I'm an angel!" I sit on the bar stool by the island.

She chuckles. "Well, Mrs. O'Connor was already sleeping when I got here this evening," she says. "I just had to stop by and get the laundry and make sure there are enough groceries for the week. I suppose I can bake your favorite cookies before I leave," she says, already opening the fridge to grab the eggs. She looks back at me and gives me a smile that makes me happy to be back home, for now anyway. "Then I'll be back next weekend to bring more food and anything else you need."

"Thanks, Marcia," I say. "Need help with the cookies?"

"You know I do. They always come out better when you help," she tells me.

So, we make chocolate chip cookies. I mix the ingredients; she takes care of the rest. And we don't talk about the shitshow from the tabloids or about mom. We sit down around the small island and Marcia excitedly tells me all about this new soap opera she is watching and by the time she is done, I'm probably all caught up on the whole storyline.

"Well, I should get going, kiddo. Are you going to be okay?" She gives me a concerned look.

I stand up to grab a drink. "I suppose I can survive house arrest for a bit," I give her a goodnight kiss on the cheek. I then turn around and open the fridge, grabbing a bottle of chocolate milk, because who doesn't need a good chocolate overdose? "Besides, everyone is quarantined anyway," I say with a shrug.

She gives me a smile that doesn't quite reach her eyes.

"Don't give Mrs. O'Connor too much trouble, you hear?"

"Yes, ma'am."

"And have another cookie before you head to bed. You look like you need it."

I chuckle and grab another.

I'm halfway through the first cookie when I get a text from Douchebag Sullivan.

"Don't forget to stream," he says. "The contract doesn't pause because you're not on tour or on house arrest."

"Fucker," I mumble under my breath.

Part of my contract with the label is that I stream something about my life at least once a day.

I sigh. I'm tired as hell, but I grab my phone, and go live as I make my way to my old room.

"Hey lovelies, so as you will likely read in a tabloid somewhere, I'm officially on house arrest," I take a bite of the chocolate chip cookie, "It's not going too bad right now, considering the mouthwatering cookies." I say as I lick my lips. Then I grin just thinking of the reactions. I put my hand on the door handle, noticing that the lights are on. I hope my room hasn't been turned into a dance studio or something crazy. "There is only one thing that could top this, and that's a beautiful-" I open the door to my room and I freeze. I realize that I'm gaping on the camera, but I keep it rolling. *'Why are there two chicks sleeping in my room?'* I think to myself. One is on the far side, facing the wall, but it is the other one – the blonde, who captures my attention. "Well," I whisper, turning the camera around as I walk toward the bed. Mesmerized by the fact that someone can look so perfect... so peaceful... while sleeping.

I zoom in on her before I turn the camera back to me and smile.

"It looks like I've found sleeping beauty."

4

(DAY 2)

RILEY

I HAVE this annoying habit of waking up five minutes before my alarm goes off. I've always been this way. Today, before I even open my eyes, I know something is different. It even smells different. Not bad – just, I don't know how to explain it – a musk scent?

I open my eyes and come face to face with Krissy, mouth hanging open, and snoring, which makes me laugh. Then I turn to the other side, and I scream as I abruptly sit up.

It's enough to wake her up too. "What the hell. What is –?" She sits up, not fully awake. She rubs her eyes and looks over to where I'm looking.

Krissy freezes as she sees a sleeping, shirtless Levi passed out on the floor, not even three feet away from the bed. He's wearing nothing but blue boxer shorts, which I'm sure is enough to make her day. He rolls to his side, facing us, and he has my sweatshirt bundled up and is using it as a pillow.

Krissy squeals an OMG in a super high pitch voice when he kicks his leg, as if that will get rid of the ankle monitor.

Levi rubs his eyes and smiles. "Who is this happy this early in the morning?" I say under my breath.

His hazel green eyes bore into mine as he says, "It's one of my special abilities. I can make anyone happy in the morning, including myself."

I tilt my head to the side and glare at him. "What the hell are you doing here?" I ask.

He yawns, still laying down, but now propping his head up. "Well, being that this is my room, I think you should be the one answering that question," he says in a playful tone.

I'm about to open my mouth when the door barges open. "Levi O'Connor. In the living room. Now!" Mrs. O'Connor yells and I don't think I've ever seen her this mad.

"Well, that didn't take long," he mumbles under his breath. He stands and grabs a white t-shirt off the chair, pulling it over his head. "Well, ladies. It's been a pleasure," he says and winks in our direction before he follows her out.

The moment he closes the door behind them, Krissy squeals again. "I just slept with Levi O'Connor!" She says and I smack my forehead.

"Come on. You can't tell me he isn't hot."

"He is," I pause. "A hot mess," I laugh as I get out of bed.

Out of habit, I grab my sweatshirt and put it on. "And by the way. Correction: you slept in the same room as him," I say with a scowl realizing that now I smell like him.

She rolls her eyes at me and laughs. "Details..." she gestures in a sweeping motion.

"Ugh. You're as bad as those tabloids. You could probably work for them."

She grins widely. "That's not a bad idea. I mean, we do have direct access to him."

I shake my head again. There is no hope for her.

"What do you think he did this time?" She asks.

"Well, considering that he likely came from jail straight here, I don't think he could've done anything new," I tell her.

"Come on, this is Levi we are talking about. Trouble is his middle name," she says as she reaches for the door.

"What the hell are you doing?"

"I'm going to work on my investigative news skills, of course," she says with a smile.

And I stupidly follow her to keep her out of trouble.

LEVI

It's been minutes, but it feels like an eternity. Part of me wants to remind her that I'm 22. Not the little kid who used to sit in this same exact chair at the kitchen island while she went on and on, and on. The sensible part of me knows that reminding her that I'm a grown ass adult would only drag the one-sided conversation out for much longer, so I just shut up and zone out, thinking of the start lyrics of a new song while that is going on.

This whole time, she's keeping her distance, and it's not until she slides her phone across the table, open on my favorite tabloid's website, that I get out of my own head.

"You need to take that video down," she warns.

On the front page of their website, there is a picture of sleeping beauty next to a picture of me.

"Could our favorite troublemaker have found love?" And "Who is Sleeping Beauty?" are highlighted in big bold letters.

'Well, the label is going to be freaking ecstatic,' I think to myself.

"We both know the damage is done," I tell mom and she glares at me.

"Shit. How old is she?" I ask, hoping I didn't just fuck up by posting a picture of a minor, although, the label would be happy about the press either way. I think.

"She just turned 18 last month. Not the point, Levi Jameson."

Fuck. The middle name. Now I'm paying attention.

"She's not even on social media," she snarls.

I chuckle. There is no way. "You are kidding, right?"

"Some people like their privacy."

I grab my phone. "I have to get permission from Sullivan to delete it. It's part of my contract," I say.

That pisses her off even more. "So you're worried about Sullivan's permission. Interesting. Did you think of asking Riley for *her* permission to blast *her* face on *your* Instagram?"

I open my Instagram. "Holy fuck. This is twice the number of views I've gotten on my highest viewed video before today," I mumble under my breath, realizing how much worse I just made this situation. And Sullivan isn't just going to say no. He is going to say fuck no.

"I don't care what Sullivan says," mom tells me. "You didn't ask her to post."

I try to get on her good side. Otherwise, these are going to be the longest 90 days of my life. "Come on, Mom. This will die down."

"I. do. not. care, Levi. You have 24 hours to make it disappear. All of it." She stares at me, likely thinking of ways to make my life a little more miserable. "You're also going to tell her. And apologize."

There it is. "Yes, Mother."

Just then, we hear a "Holy crap," coming from the hallway.

"Well, now is as good of a time as any," mom says, followed by, "Krissy. Riley, come here, please."

They come around the corner then. Her friend pokes her head around the corner first and she has this look in her eyes that I see at every show. Sleeping Beauty on the other hand – well, she is pissed.

I wave at them.

"Levi, this is Riley and Krissy," mom says, then she crosses her arms over her chest and starts tapping her foot.

"Hi," I say. "It seems that I owe you an apology, Sleeping Beauty," I say with a grin.

"Levi!" Mom scowls.

"Riley. My name is Riley," she says, sounding infuriated.

"I'm sorry, Riley. I shouldn't have done that. I was just… I was just in the middle of streaming and I was caught off guard. I sent a message to my manager to see if we can get it taken down."

"Thank you," she says.

Her friend speaks up then, looking up from her phone, and that fangirl look in her eyes is gone. "Soooo… hmmm… there are these fake profiles with girls claiming to be sleeping beauty, but using her picture, and –"

"Shit. I'll have the PR team take care of it. You're really not on social media at all?" I ask curiously.

"Nope," she says in a cold tone.

Ouch. "Okay. That's good, or bad. Depending on how you look at it. Crap."

"Definitely bad. There's no good about it, considering that people are trying to impersonate me."

Aaaand she is on the verge of tears. Damnit. She is right. I nod. "I'll take care of it." I glance at mom and she nods her approval. I reach forward, grab the tray of cookies and offer it to her.

"Cookie?" I ask. "They do have a reputation of making everything better."

Without thinking, I stand and bring the tray near them so she can reach for one.

"Levi!" mom yells, and I realize how I just fucked up again.

"Do you know how bad things are overseas? Not to mention you just got back from a concert with who knows how many people around. Not to mention jail."

"Mom," I say in a calming tone. "It will be fine! You know how the news exaggerates things." I point toward myself. "Exhibit A. Besides, we've been under the same roof for hours now. I think it's a little late to be cautious."

Mom audibly sighs and Sleeping Beauty stalks out of the room.

5

RILEY

I BARGE into his room with every intention of grabbing my things and going back to Carly's bedroom. At least until she gets here. But the moment I step inside his room and spot his guitar on the floor, next to my dance shoes, I freeze, and tears of frustration well up in my eyes. It hits me that the shoes represent everything that I am. And his guitar makes me think of everything I never got to experience because of it. I love what I do. I couldn't imagine doing anything else. But because of it, I never made the time to go to concerts, to go to parties... and now, I may never – "Riley, are you okay?" I hear Krissy ask me as she closes the door behind us, but her voice sounds muffled. I feel my heart pounding against my chest, faster and faster, as I start to gasp for air.

I put my hand over my chest.

I can't breathe.

I can't.

"Riley!" Krissy screams. I can barely hear her, and I can't say anything. I just face her and continue to gasp for air. I start to feel hot. Krissy rushes toward me with a water bottle she grabbed from the nightstand, but I can't – I just – I move my hands to my neck, feeling like I'm suffocating. My chest is pounding so hard it hurts. At some point, I think I hear Krissy scream for help, and next thing I know, Levi is standing in front of me.

He puts his hands on each side of my face, and I can barely see him in between the tears and the coughs and gasps.

"Close your eyes," I hear the faint sound of his voice. He moves in closer and leans toward my right. I feel his breath against my neck. "Close your eyes, Riley," he says into my ear.

My breath catches, causing me to gasp again. But I do as he said. I close my eyes and I feel tears run down my face.

"Take a deep breath... one... another... two... another... three..." My heart is still pounding, but the pain is not as intense. The sound of his voice is louder now. "... another... four." I gasp for air again and start to open my eyes. He doesn't let go of me. "Keep your eyes closed, Riley. Imagine that you are at the studio. Alone." He rubs his thumbs back and forth right below my ears in a way that practically demands that my breathing matches the slow pace of his movements. "Deep breath. The sun is shining on you through the windows. Breathe. There is music. Think of your favorite song. Breathe. Deep breaths. Good."

He lets go of me then, and I slowly open my eyes and

find him staring down at me, his brows furrowed as he bites his lip, looking concerned. Next to him, Krissy has her arms wrapped around Mrs. O'Connor, eyes widened in shock and lips quivering. She looks terrified. Mrs. O'Connor looks just as concerned, and she's holding out her phone ready to call 911.

Levi hands me the bottle of water. "Drink this," he says.

I do. I take one sip, then put it down. "I'm sorry," I tell Krissy.

"You don't have to apologize," she says. "What happened?"

"Panic attack," Levi answers for me. "Has it ever happened before?" He asks.

I nod, "A couple of times," I answer, thinking of the first, when mom told me about Aunt Lilly's diagnosis.

"How did you know what to do?" I ask him as I sit on the edge of the bed. Krissy rushes to my side, sitting next to me and pulling me toward her into a side hug. I've had these attacks before, but never this bad. And I don't know what would've happened if he didn't know exactly what to do. His tone is softer and serious. "One of the guys from the band has panic attacks every once in a while."

"Oh." I pause, looking up at him. "Th-thank you," I stammer.

My phone rings then, and I pick it up thinking maybe it's my mom. Still distraught by what just happened, I answer without thinking.

"Hi mom."

"Hi. Is this Riley Andrews?"

"Yes. Who is this?"

"Can you give a statement about the sleeping beauty video? Are you dating Levi O'Connor?"

At first, I look helplessly at Levi, mostly because I feel like I'm still in shock, and the call doesn't help. He gives me a puzzled look and I swallow the lump in my throat.

"How did you get this number??" I ask, alarmed.

I stand up as I put the phone on speaker.

The person on the phone doesn't answer. He keeps pressing as if I didn't even say anything at all. "How long have you been together? I just need confirmation that you are in fact dating."

Mrs. O'Connor glares at Levi and he just shakes his head, then gives me this apologetic look. Levi slowly reaches for the phone and ends the call, then turns to face her.

"Yes, I get it, mother. I fucked up again."

"Levi," Mrs. O'Connor says. "I think it's best if you stay in Carly's room for now. And please take care of that situation."

He nods once and walks toward the door, grabbing his guitar on the way out.

LEVI

'Damn reporters.' I think to myself as I flop down on the bed.

I hold her phone up and block his number, then text Sullivan saying we need to talk.

There will be other calls, but I'll just block them too. At least until she realizes I have her phone.

Bored, I look through her playlist. There is a lot you can tell about someone based on their playlists. She only has one, and it has nothing but 5 songs on it. 'Hmmm. Mysterious.' I grin when I see the one most played. Classical music. But that is most definitely not what makes me smile.

I composed that when I was seventeen.

Deciding not to go down memory lane, I grab the remote, turn the TV on and grab two pillows, propping my head up. After switching through three different channels featuring nothing but news about lockdowns, masks, and pandemic, I finally settle on old reruns of *Friends*.

I'm on the second episode when I look at the time. Eleven in the morning. These are going to be the longest 90 days of my life.

I call Bentley.

"Hey, man."

"Hey," I say in a monotone voice. "What are you doing?"

"Hmmm waking up," he says with a yawn. "Why?"

"No reason." I say as I sit up. "I'm bored," I continue to scroll through her phone. I'm curious and I want to look through her pictures, but it doesn't feel right. "Figured I'd live vicariously through you."

"Wow," he says.

"What?"

"Dude. You do not need to live through me. Have you seen your Instagram? And who is sleeping beauty??" He asks excitedly.

"It doesn't matter. She can't stand me," I put him on

speaker, throw the phone on the bed and reach for my guitar.

"Uh huh. How is house arrest anyway? They treating you okay?"

"Fucker. Well, considering my mom is here and one of her students who is staying with us can't stand me, it's safe to assume that jail would've been better."

He chuckles, and I know I made a mistake saying that. "Soooo, sleeping beauty is your mom's student. I like where this is going."

I let out a sigh. "Yeah… Again, she can't stand me, so it is literally not going anywhere." I start playing the guitar and Bentley is quiet for a moment.

"So make her like you," he says, and I stop, still keeping my fingers in place. Certainly you can do something insanely idiotic to make that happen. It always works."

"I doubt it will work on her, man. She's different."

"Uh oh."

"Uh oh what?"

"Nothing. I mean… sounds like we'll be getting new songs soon. Just don't make them all sappy and shit."

"Fuck you," I say with a laugh. "Hey, come over later, okay? I'm bored out of my mind."

"You do know there is a lockdown in place, right?" He asks.

"Yeah. So, are you coming or what?"

"I'll be there in about an hour or two."

The moment I hang up, her phone rings.

Out of town number. Yeah, I'm ready to cuss out a few reporters today.

I put the guitar to the side, ready to go off. I don't care what the press says about me, but this is overboard. I lean back against the headboard. "Hello?" I answer.

"Hi, I'm calling for Riley Andrews?" The woman says, as if trying to find out if this is her phone.

"Where are you calling from?"

The line goes silent.

"I'm with the Happy Paws Vacation Spot," she finally says.

'Well, they're getting creative,' I think to myself.

"This is Levi O'Connor," I say. "How can I help you?"

There is a long pause again.

"As in, the Levi O'Connor?" She asks.

"The one and only. I think. How can I be of service?" I ask and she giggles. Okay, reporters don't usually do that.

"Well, I'm helping out with the boarding place where her lab is staying, but we have to close down. We need her to arrange for someone to pick him up by the end of business today."

"And end of business is..."

"At five," she replies.

I glance at the area code and do a quick search on my phone. Charleston, South Carolina number.

"Are you in Charleston? I ask.

"Near Charleston."

"Wow. Okay. So, close down because of the lockdown?" I ask, confused. I mean, they should still be able to care for the pets.

"Actually, all of the staff members got sick. Two are in the hospital because of the virus. And I don't even work here. I have to leave town today to take care of my grandma."

I sit up straighter. This is insane. "What happens if people don't have someone to pick up their pets by then?"

"Well," she sighs and starts sobbing on the phone. *'Great going, Levi,'* I think to myself. 'Just go on making every female around cry today.'

"We have to send them to a shelter," she sobs. "Which I hate. We just don't see another option. Every other boarding place near us is either closing or full, and –"

"I'm sorry. What was your name?"

"Sarah."

"Sarah, I have an idea..."

"Okay."

When I hang up with her, I text Bentley.

Me: So, something insanely idiotic, huh?

Bentley: Yep.

Me: I got it. But I'm going to need your help. Do you think Johnny is still around?

Bentley: As in Johnny the pilot?

Me: Yep.

Bentley: God. I'm afraid to ask... What you got?

Me: I'm gonna call you.

6

RILEY

"WHAT HAPPENED?" Krissy asks as we both sit down on the bed, side by side. I grab a pillow and hold it tightly against my chest. "Stress, I think," My hands start to tremble, and I hold the pillow tighter, tucking my hands in so Krissy doesn't notice it. "It just all hit me at once, you know?" I sigh. "The unknown. The lockdown, the virus." I start to choke up, "The fact that it could end my aunt's life even faster than the doctor's prognosis." I wipe the tears with the back of my hand. "Heck, I could die and I haven't even really lived or experienced anything," I sigh again. "Not knowing what will happen with our audition, that stupid video and how that could impact me getting a scholarship." I pause and avoid her gaze. "Should I go on?"

Krissy puts a hand on my shoulder. "Riley, it's not like that video was something scandalous. You didn't do anything wrong."

Mrs. O'Connor clears her throat from the door and

we look in her direction. "She's right, Riley. And the audition will just be pushed back for two weeks until lockdown is over. It'll go by fast," she tells me. "It will be okay."

"But what if –"

"I know it's hard," she cuts me off, and in a calm tone, she says, "try not to stress over the what ifs. Just focus on dancing. Think of it as extra time to practice," she says offering a warm smile. "Now, I have to get on the road to pick-up Carly. I'm already running behind. But please call me if there are any problems with Levi, okay? I'll be back the day after tomorrow. Marcia will be stopping by tonight to check on things. On Levi specifically," she rolls her eyes. "Do you mind being around to make sure Levi doesn't ask her to run any extra unnecessary errands or anything? She would let him get away with murder," she sighs.

"Okay," Krissy and I both say at the same time.

When Mrs. O'Connor leaves, I face Krissy. "I have to admit. I'm surprised you're not gushing all over him, especially about the way he handled my panic attack and all."

"That was pretty scary, Riley. I'm so freaking glad he was here and helped you through it; but to be honest, the whole 'relaxed and don't care attitude' doesn't do it for me."

"Sometimes I wish I could be a little like that," I say truthfully.

"What do you mean?"

"I guess I just stress too much about every little thing. I don't know what it is like not to worry about it all, or just live in the moment and not worry about the what ifs."

I sigh, and move the pillow, looking around. "Talking about worrying... have you seen my phone?"

LEVI

I'm laying on the bed, throwing a tennis ball up in the air, while I talk to Bentley on the phone. Mom opens the door and I quickly sit up, grab the phone from the bed and take him off speaker.

"Hold on," I tell him.

"Ever heard of knocking?" I ask. "I mean, I could have a girl in here. Maybe more and we could be –" I start to say in a playful tone, but she cuts me off. "No, you couldn't. And you won't. And tell Bentley I said hello," she says. I can hear Bentley laughing. "I'm going to drive down to pick-up Carly. You can stay in her room until we get back. After that, you get the couch."

"Ouch," I say as I put my hands over my heart.

She stares at me, studying my every move. "You look like you're plotting something. Don't," she warns.

"What makes you think that?" I ask giving her what I think is one of my most innocent smiles. It doesn't work.

"Oh, I know!" Some things just never change," she says in an annoyed tone. "Well, I have to go." She points at me like I'm a little kid. "I have eyes on you, Levi Jameson."

"Always," I smirk.

The moment she leaves the room, I'm back on the phone.

"Okay, so there is one more thing," I tell Bentley.

"I don't get it. Why don't you just tell her they called. Maybe she has someone local who can go pick-up the dog."

"What if she doesn't?" I ask.

"Then we make that our plan B," he suggests.

I run my fingers through my hair and sigh. "Look. Honestly, I don't think she can deal with the stress right now. Besides, you specifically told me to do something insanely idiotic."

"Ha! I didn't tell you that. I suggested it. Which means if you decide to do it I'm not responsible."

"Well, it is decided. And like I said, there is one more thing."

He hesitates. "What?"

I stand up and start pacing. He's not going to like this. "I need you to wait until they close. And bring back all pets they have left."

"What? Why?" he asks in an alarmed tone.

"Because we can't let them be sent to a shelter. That's why. Just make sure the boarding place has my phone number. We'll give the pets back if the owners claim them. However long it takes. We'll just foster them."

"Dude!" He warns.

"They have one other dog and a cat staying. That's not many."

"It's enough for your mom to kill you. And who is going to take care of them when that happens?" He jokes.

"You," I say with a grin.

"And if the owners don't claim them?" he asks.

"Then I keep them," I tell him.

He laughs and I can picture him shaking his head.

"And when we go on tour?"

"Marcia can puppy-sit," I say. "Keep it coming. I have an answer for everything, as always."

"Fine. Yeah. You're right. We both know I would never leave them to fend for themselves. I suppose the guys and I can take the other dog and cat," he offers, and I'm not surprised.

"Alright. Thanks, Bentley. You know I'd do it myself but –"

"Yeah, yeah… that rough house arrest life."

I hear someone knocking on the bedroom door, and I swear, my fucking heartbeat races. *'What the hell?'* I think to myself.

"Hey, I gotta go."

7

LEVI

PART of me hopes to open the door to find Riley standing there; but instead, there is her friend with her arms crossed over her chest. Her awesome blue highlights distracting me from that 'I mean business' look in her eyes.

"Hi. Do you have Riley's phone?" she asks, already extending her hand because she knows I have it. I give her a smile. She doesn't return it. *'These girls are tough.'* I think to myself. I gotta say, the fans have spoiled me over the years. This… I won't put up with your BS attitude Riley and her friend seem to have is a little – well, real and refreshing, to be honest.

Thankful that I thought of deleting the call from the boarding place, I walk over to the bed, grab her phone, and walk back to the door, extending it to her.

She reaches for the phone, but I smile and pull it away.

"Krissy, right?" I ask, and she nods. "What is her deal?" I ask, tilting my head toward my old bedroom door.

She gives me a puzzled look.

"The no social media thing, the panic attack?"

She shrugs and looks from me to her extended hand, palm facing up to ask for the phone. "She doesn't like distractions. Dancing is her life, and she's damn good at it," she pauses, lowering her hand. "She has spent her whole life preparing for this audition in the hopes of getting into her dream school, and now she needs a scholarship on top of that, so," her eyes widen as she catches herself and stops.

I raise a brow at her. "She didn't need a scholarship before? What changed?"

She takes in a deep breath, getting annoyed and I hand her the phone. She snatches the phone from my hand and shoves it in her back pocket. "That is not my business to share. But the whole thing with social media needs to disappear. She's worried that all those dumbasses trying to impersonate her are going to mess up her chances. You know, if the school or the scholarship committee happen to look her up."

"Okay, I get that, but if they're really giving that much value to social media instead of her talent, they have problems," I say.

Krissy chuckles. "You most definitely don't get it."

I shake my head, and give in. "Fine. Fair enough. But I do have an idea. Do you think she will hear me out?"

"Riley!" Krissy yells at the top of her lungs as she walks toward the living room.

I follow her. Riley comes out of the bedroom wearing

a black leotard, sheer black skirt-thingie, and pink ballet shoes, and she exudes confidence as she makes her way to us. Her posture, the way she walks, the way she looks at me without shying away… it's all breathtaking and quite unexpected.

"Levi has something he'd like to propose," Krissy says as she hands sleeping beauty her phone.

They both sit on the couch. Krissy slouches back and Riley sits up straight as she starts to look through her phone.

"I'm going to grab a snack. Anyone want anything?" I ask, heading toward the kitchen.

When I look back for a response, Krissy shakes her head, giving me an impatient look, while sleeping beauty continues to look at her phone.

"Okay, okay. We'll talk first." I sit on the recliner across from them. "Alright, so this whole thing with the video… I have a solution. Taking it down won't make things go away. It's everywhere now."

"Not helping," Krissy says, rolling her eyes.

Riley is still staring at her phone, and I have a feeling that is just to avoid looking at me. I notice Riley's knuckles are white as she tightens her grip on her phone. Maybe she feels me watching her, because she looks at me then, and I see the concern in Riley's eyes. *'Okay, so that really didn't help,'* I think to myself.

"Don't worry. I have a solution," I lean back in the recliner. "We can't make it go away, but we can take control of the situation – take charge of the narrative."

Riley chuckles, "Because you do that soooo well."

I'm caught completely off guard by her comeback, and I grin. "Ouch. You girls have zero mercy."

"Okay, tell me how?" She asks in a serious tone.

"Just hear me out, okay? We set up your own social media. Get the account verified, so that if colleges look you up, they'll know it's the real you. And you're controlling the content."

I smile, looking damn proud of my master plan, but Riley just looks lost and confused, and for a second, I wonder how much she even knows about social media.

As Riley continues to sit quietly, Krissy interjects, leaning forward. "They're just gonna think she's one of the many Rileys now that they know her name. Us peasants can't just get an account verified like your highness," she gestures toward me.

I laugh. I like her friend. Snarky and loyal. She reminds me of Bentley. In fact, she's just the type of person Bentley needs to meet. The poor guy has the worst luck when it comes to girls.

"I can help with that," I say, looking at Riley. "I can tag you. Hell, if you want, I can set up everything and you don't even have to see it."

"I don't want anyone to assume that we're in a relationship," she blurts out, staring right at me, but she looks distant.

"Why?" I ask, confused, knowing that other women would die for this.

"I don't want the scholarship committee thinking that I'm surrounded by distractions."

"Distractions?" I ask.

Krissy rolls her eyes at me. "Let's face it… no offense, but your life is a circus. According to the tabloids, just the other day you were sleeping with some politician's daughter while her boyfriend was being distracted backstage."

"Aw. You were reading about me," I joke, but I notice that sleeping beauty is crinkling her nose, giving me this disgusted look, and I hate it.

"That's not what actually happened. You do know they sometimes like to manipulate and fictionalize things to get readers, right?"

Riley avoids my gaze as Krissy crosses her arms over her chest.

"I can say that you are a –"

"Friend?" Krissy suggests.

I shake my head. "It won't work. It will just fuel people's imaginations. They see what they want to see."

Krissy faces sleeping beauty.

"Riley, do you trust me?"

"Most of the time," she jokes, and I see a hint of a smile again. Ah that smile. I need to see more of that and less of that lost look in her eyes.

"Let him do this, say what he wants to say, tag you, and then he can do some unrelated idiotic thing as a distraction so his groupies will focus on that instead."

I can't even be mad. She isn't wrong, and yeah, she definitely needs to meet Bentley. I can't quit grinning as she goes on and on with this master plan.

Krissy shifts in her seat and I can see a spark in her eyes that wasn't there before. "Or better yet!" she says excitedly. "Pretend that you're dating for a few days. A week tops! Then fake a breakup. That's the quickest way for people to move on," she shrugs.

Riley bites her bottom lip. "I just don't want to see any of it. One week and I want this all gone."

My heartbeat races at the thought of fake dating her for a few days.

'What is happening to me?' I feel like a hormonal teenager.

But she still doesn't look happy. She looks uneasy.

"You know," I say, looking at her. "If the people from the school are really looking at your social media, it will help to have pictures and videos of you dancing."

She looks at Krissy, looking completely out of her element.

"The boy is not wrong," Krissy says with a shrug.

"Boy?" I ask, raising my voice. "Man," I correct her and she rolls her eyes, which makes me laugh.

"I can help take the shots," I offer as I stand up and stretch my back. I catch a glimpse of Riley looking when my shirt rises up. *'Maybe not all hope is lost after all.'* I think to myself. "It's the least I can do, plus I'm bored out of my mind."

She doesn't answer right away.

"I'll have to think about it."

"Okay, and before I forget, I have one requirement," I say, staring into her brown eyes.

"What?" She asks nervously.

"As my girlfriend for the week," I grin. "I get to call you sleeping beauty."

8

RILEY

"HEY MOM," I answer the phone, putting it up against the back of the kitchen counter as I finish clearing mine and Krissy's dinner plates.

"Hey, sweetheart," Mom says in a concerned tone that matches her expression.

I immediately stop what I'm doing and pick-up the phone. "Is Aunt Lilly okay?" I ask when I realize it's not even morning there yet.

"Yeah. She is good. We're in Thailand now. We were lucky they haven't banned incoming international flights yet. I think it's coming though. Most places are closed, but we're making the best of it. I'm just worried about being able to go back home, that is all," she pauses. "I think we may have to stay longer until it's safe for her to travel."

"Makes sense." I sit on the couch next to Krissy. She grabs the blue nail polish that matches her highlights and tells me to prop my feet up. Mrs. O'Connor has a strict no nail polish rule. She likes things to look uniform. Black leotards, pink shoes, buns… no extras. So I get why Krissy is taking the opportunity to do this while Mrs. O'Connor is away.

"Do you already know what will happen to the audition?" Mom asks. "You look a little – drained," she says, studying me.

I try my best to put on a smile so she won't worry. "Yeah. Mrs. O'Connor said they will probably just push it back two weeks."

"Are you sure it's okay for you to stay with her until then? Maybe I should talk to her."

"Mom, it's okay. I promise. Mrs. O'Connor says it's more than fine. And you have plenty to worry about already. Just focus on Aunt Lilly, okay?"

She smiles back at me. "How did I get so lucky?"

I notice Marcia come in then, carrying a huge bag of dog food and a few small grocery bags.

"What in the world is that boy up to?" She asks as she manages to put everything down on the floor.

My mom looks confused, and the last thing I want to do right now is to explain Levi O'Connor to her.

"Mom, I have to help with the groceries. I'll call you back, okay?"

"Wait!" She stops me. "Boy? What boy?"

Krissy is giggling next to me and it's hard to keep myself from rolling my eyes at her.

"No one," I say dismissively, trying to rush her off the phone. "It's just Mrs. O'Connor's son. I have to go though. I love you. Tell Aunt Lilly I said hi."

"Love you too."

I hang up the phone and make sure my nails are dry before I go help Marcia.

"Dog food?" I ask, confused.

"Exactly," she says as she motions her hands up in the air. "Mr. Levi didn't get a dog, did he?"

"No," I say.

"Where is he anyway?" She asks.

"In Carly's room, I think."

She sighs. "Well, I'll deal with him later. Mrs. O'Connor called. We have a surprise for you girls."

"Oh?" I say surprised as Krissy bolts from her seat. She loves surprises. I typically hate them.

We follow Marcia, looking confused as we're led out of the apartment. Then she presses the button for the elevator.

"Should we have grabbed masks?" I ask.

"Dammit. I keep forgetting it," she quickly pulls a mask out of her pocket and puts it on. "You'll be okay. I'm wearing one and you haven't been anywhere."

"Okay," I tell her nervously. It's only been a few days, but it feels awkward being outside of the apartment. We get in the elevator, she scans a card, presses a button that looks a bit different from the others, and the elevator goes up. I'm even more confused now.

Then the elevator door opens to an open area with tables and chairs. On the side closest to the elevator, there is a bar, and on the side past the tables and chairs, there is the entrance to a garden, surrounded by small lights hanging everywhere.

"What's this?" I ask.

"Just something that the building's owner has been

working on. He's going to open a rooftop garden and bar for residents and guests soon. Mrs. O'Connor arranged to have this space so you girls can practice. You can just move the tables and chairs to the side, and you got yourselves a nice dance floor. The only downside is that the owner is Bentley's dad, so the boys have been known to practice here when they're not on tour."

Krissy and I take one look around.

"Can we stay here now?" I ask, eager to dance in peace and quiet.

"The place is yours whenever you want it," Marcia grins as Krissy and I rush to move the tables and chairs out of the way.

LEVI

I'm taking a nap in Carly's room when Bentley calls me.

"DUDE!" Bentley yells into my ear, and I pull the phone away, squinting. "We have a HUGE problem! HUGE!"

I'm definitely awake now. "What?" I ask in a calm tone.

"Did you know that the other dog is a Great Dane? This dog is a horse!"

"Okay, so we'll buy more food. And why do you sound like you're out of breath?"

"You don't understand. I cannot fit Cupcake in my tiny little car. I tried. Hence why I'm out of breath."

"Wait." I laugh. "The Great Dane's name is Cupcake? I'd say that is the real problem."

"Ha. That's just wrong, isn't it?" He jokes. "Anyway. I need help getting him home before I bring you Riley's dog and I have a plan, but you're not gonna like it."

"What you got?" I ask.

"Okay, so... someone... likely Lucifer, I mean – my douchebag brother," he refers to Sullivan, "called that one paparazzi that seems to be everywhere we go. He has a van, and he's offering to help me out if you give him an interview about the situation at the show and your arrest."

I hesitate. I could care less about the interview part, but I don't want him near Riley or Krissy.

"Hang on a minute," I tell him, putting him on speaker as I text the lawyer – yes, he's a family friend and I have him on speed dial.

Me: Hey. Does my paperwork say whether I can go as far as the rooftop?

Lawyer: Yes. Cabin fever already?

Me: Something like that.

"Okay," I tell Bentley. "Bring her lab –"

"Wilson," Bentley corrects me. "If you're trying to impress the girl, you gotta know the dog's name. And the dog pretty much has to approve. Just so you know."

I chuckle. "Okay. Good thing pets love me." I pause. "Anyway. Take the guy to the rooftop for the interview. Then bring Wilson to the apartment alone."

"Alright then," he says. "I'm dropping off Cupcake and Whiskers first."

"Whiskers? Who named these pets?" I ask, changing into my ripped jeans and black shirt.

"Exactly," Bentley says with a chuckle. "Anyway. Max's mom is going to our place to watch Cupcake and Whiskers. I'm bringing the guys over with me for moral support."

"Fine. Remember – the paparazzi goes straight to the rooftop. I don't want him anywhere near Riley."

9

LEVI

'It's her smile," I think to myself, sitting on the bed and holding my guitar. *'That has to be it.'* I try to reason why I can't get her out of my head. She doesn't smile often. I wish she did. But when she does, it's never fake – like I so often do. It's with reason, and somehow, that makes that moment even more valuable.

Right now, I stay in Carly's room because I know that if I go out there and see Riley, I'll end up giving it away that we're bringing her dog here. It has to be a surprise. I smile, anticipating her reaction. I'm barely able to contain myself, just waiting on the message from Bentley, so I do one of the things that makes me feel relaxed.

I put the guitar down on the bed, grab a notebook, and start scribbling lyrics down.

I thought I was just broken
Destined to fake the smile

Leave it all unspoken
Mind running mile after mile

And then, the text comes.

"Here. Lucifer's minion is upstairs. I'm outside the apartment."

I rush to the door and open it to find a tired looking Bentley – down to dark circles under his eyes and wrinkled black shirt covered with dog hair. "What happened to you?" I ask and he tilts his head toward a very excited chocolate lab. Bentley lets go of Wilson's leash, and he charges at me.

I pet Wilson. "I guess he likes you," Bentley says, walking toward the kitchen and opening the fridge. "I don't know if I'm more hungry, tired, or horny."

I laugh. "I can only help with two of those things."

Bentley peeks over the side of the refrigerator door. "Which ones?" he grins, and I shake my head.

"Ohhhh No. No. No!" I turn to find Marcia coming from my mom's room holding cleaning supplies in both hands. A scowl on her face.

At first, I think she's talking about Bentley rampaging the fridge, but then I notice she is looking at Wilson, who is patiently sitting next to me.

I smile at her. "I can explain."

"Please do," she tells me, putting the cleaning supplies on the table and crossing her arms.

"This is Riley's dog," I say in a whisper as I approach her. "They were going to send him to a shelter because of the lockdown. You know I couldn't let that happen," I pout.

Her expression softens and she shakes her head.

"Your mother is going to kill you."

"Yeah, I know."

Marcia sighs, looking at Wilson. Then she smiles. "If she gives you trouble, you call me. I'll come get him and Riley."

I pull her into a hug. "And this is why you're my favorite person in the world," I say.

"Yeah, yeah…" She rolls her eyes and pets the dog. "What's his name?"

"Wilson," I pause. "Is Riley in my room?" I ask, turning around to see Bentley making himself comfortable on the couch. I give it five minutes before he's out.

"Nah. Your mom talked to Mr. Sullivan about the girls using the rooftop to practice."

My stomach drops. "Shit!"

I look at Marcia. "Please watch him for a bit," I say as I rush out of the apartment.

RILEY

Krissy and I are taking a break, standing by the bar when the elevator door opens. The man, who looks to be in his thirties, wearing jeans and a faded t-shirt, hesitates, then starts walking toward us. He swings a backpack over his shoulder. "Sorry to interrupt," he says, putting his hair up in a manbun. "Just here to do inventory." He keeps his distance, walking behind the bar.

"Okay. We'll be out of your way." I say and I start to head toward the elevator, hoping Krissy will follow me, when he clears his throat, stopping us. "They were about to do maintenance. Said the elevator would be running again in about 15 minutes."

"Thank you," I say politely, pulling Krissy toward the bench at the garden's entrance instead. I lean in toward her, rubbing my hands up and down my arms.

"That guy is giving me the creeps," I whisper.

"Relax," Krissy says as she drinks from a water bottle she grabbed from the mini fridge earlier. "He looks like he's actually doing inventory," she says.

I peek out of the corner of my eyes and he is leaning down, glancing under the counter.

"Yeah, but the place isn't even open yet. Did you see a lot of things back there when you got the water?"

Krissy quickly glances at him. "Well, no, but maybe... well, I wasn't really paying attention," she says with a puzzled expression. "Do you want to go into the garden, away from him?"

"Yes and no," I tell her. "I think my paranoid self would rather stay where we can see him."

We hear the elevator ding and chills crawl up my arms as I wonder if he lied about maintenance or if it was just delayed. I glance in that direction to see Levi, and I let out a breath, feeling myself relax. Levi on the other hand, looks the opposite of relaxed, which seems unusual for him. His face is red, fists clenched, and his eyes are widened as he looks around, and then, he spots the man behind the bar and he charges toward him.

I grab on to Krissy's arm and freeze as we watch the man hop over the bar with a camera in hand. The man is not quick enough. Levi grabs him by the collar of his shirt, and the guy, instead of protecting himself, twists his arm back to protect the camera.

"She's off limits!" Levi growls, and the man grins.

The man isn't fazed at all by Levi. He leans his head to the side, looking at me. "You are Sleeping Beauty, right? Give me a live interview and you can have the pictures."

Levi just shakes his head, tightens his grip on the guy's shirt, and starts pulling the other hand back into a clenched fist. I instinctively find myself rushing toward him as I hear the elevator door again.

"Levi, no!" I say, my voice sounding strong in a way that surprises myself considering that a minute ago, my whole body was shaking at the thought that this guy had been here taking our pictures without us realizing it.

Levi stops and looks at me confused for a second, but doesn't let go of the guy.

I put a hand on Levi's arm, feeling his warmth under my hand.

"Let him go. Please. You're on house arrest for God's sake. You can't quite go around punching people, Levi."

The man grins again as Levi slowly lets go, and to my surprise, he slips his hand into mine, holding it tightly. I notice then that one of his bandmates… not sure which, is standing next to me.

The paparazzi straightens his shirt and smirks. "She's right. And I won't even press charges if she is part of the interview."

Levi tries to let go of my hand, but I won't let him. I get in between him and the man, and I face Levi, resting my hand against his chest.

"Fuck. That's not cool, man," his bandmate says.

Levi is still trying to inch forward.

"Look at me," I tell him. His eyes focus on me as I feel his chest rise and fall under my hand, and it doesn't take long before his breathing slows to normal. The intensity in the way he looks at me makes my breath catch, and then I feel his hand on my waist and for a moment, it feels like we're the only two on the rooftop.

The moment is gone when the flash goes off, but I continue to hold his gaze.

"Look, I'm sorry, alright?" The man says, but it's obvious he doesn't mean it. "With this whole lockdown bullshit, things are going to be slow for at least two weeks. I got bills to pay."

"Fine," Levi says, still looking into my eyes. "Let's get this over with, but she is off limits."

"She stays," the man commands, "but you can answer all the questions."

I bite my bottom lip. "It's fine," I tell Levi.

I realize then I'm wearing nothing but high waist yoga pants and a sports bra. Levi notices too.

"Bentley, can she have your shirt?"

Without saying a word, Bentley takes off his black t-shirt, which has the name of their band on it, and hands it to me. I pull it over my head and start to pick at the dog hair on it, which makes me miss my dog, Wilson.

"Are you really sure?" Levi asks, brushing a lock of my hair behind my ear – pulling my attention back to him, and I nod before we're thrown into the lion's den.

10

LEVI

"Where are the guys?" I ask Bentley as Brock, the paparazzi from hell, moves some chairs around to set things up.

"They're coming." He raises a brow at me and then narrows his gaze to my hand, holding on to Riley's. "Later" I mouth to him.

Holding on to her like this, without her pulling away, feels… comforting. The way she was able to pull me from a full-on moment of anger and calm me within seconds was just – she grounds me, and I love that she has this impact on me.

Riley is talking to Krissy as they look at Krissy's bright pink phone. I look over her shoulder and realize that Krissy is setting up an Instagram account for Riley.

"Lucifer is going to flip. You know that, right?" Bentley says, hopping on the barstool near us. I shrug. "Yeah. I know." Sullivan likes to profit from every single interview, so we're going to catch hell for this, but he'll get over it.

"Ready?" Brock interrupts, calling from where he stands. I've come across hundreds of paparazzi. Some are really nice, actually. This guy… he gives me the worst vibe.

"As I will ever be," I say in a cold tone as I lead Riley to the two chairs he set up in front of the garden's entrance.

I let go of her hand then, moving my hand to the small of her back as I lean in. "Are you good with this?" I whisper into her ear, catching the exact second when she shivers.

"Yeah," she says. Then she looks at me and grins. "Krissy is going live at the same time. This guy doesn't get to be a prick and fully benefit from it too."

I smirk, moving a lock of her hair back behind her ear. Her breath catches and she blushes. Out of the corner of my eyes, I catch Brock glaring and smirking, so I pull away. I get this gut feeling and I know without a doubt this guy is here for all the wrong reasons.

We sit down, and Brock sits across from us, and looks into his phone.

"Good evening, everyone! This is Brock Davis, and I am live with Levi O'Connor and his mysterious sleeping beauty."

I should be looking toward his phone, which is now set on the table next to him and pointing at us, but instead, I'm looking at her. She's looking straight at the camera, and I can hear her taking slow, deep breaths. I instinctively reach for her hands, clasped together on her lap and I put my hand over hers. She is freezing, making me realize just how tense she is. She isn't used to any of this, and I hate that she is in this situation because of me.

"So, Levi," he starts to say, and I feel my phone buzzing. It's undoubtedly Sullivan, and pissing him off is the one and only perk coming from this interview. "It seems that one day, you were backstage sleeping with a politician's daughter, and the next, you find who seems to be the love of your life. Can you tell us a little about that?" He cuts right to the chase.

'What.The.Fuck.' I think to myself.

I notice Riley trying to pull her hands from under mine. When she moves, I hold on to one of her hands, lacing my fingers through hers.

I want to punch him in the face, but instead, I smile and focus on clearing a few things up. I don't typically give a shit about these interviews and say what they want to hear, but not today.

"Well, Brock. Things weren't quite what they seem."

"Is that so?" He asks with a smug look in his face. "So you're telling me you didn't sleep with her? I mean, if not, that was some good photoshop done on a few of the magazines."

I bite on the inside of my cheek and count to three.

"I admit that I've made some questionable choices in the past, but no. We didn't sleep together. We did –" I look down and shake my head. I let go of Riley's hand because it doesn't even feel right to have the privilege of holding her hand while I'm talking about this. That is the moment I realize just how much she's getting to me, and for a moment, I lose my train of thought. "We were… hmmm hooking up," I say, flustered. "But that is in the past. I'm not the same person I was a few days ago."

Brock chuckles. He actually chuckles! On air, and to say that I'm annoyed is an understatement. "We'll get back to that in a minute. What I want to know is, how did the guy – the woman's boyfriend – come into the picture?"

"He got jealous and tried to give her a little payback by forcing himself on her friend right outside of the room backstage. I heard her friend struggling and did what I had to do to stop him."

"And doing what you had to do involved a knife?" He asks.

"He grabbed the knife off the snack tray backstage – near the door. I took it from him. That was when their local security showed up. I got arrested, and you know the rest."

"Okay. So, you say that you changed… in a matter of days…" he shakes his head and I glance at Riley, noticing how uncomfortable she is as she fidgets with the hem of Bentley's t-shirt. Brock looks at Riley, cocking his head to the side, studying her as he smirks. "Tell us about your mysterious girl," he asks without taking his gaze off her. "You've never been in a relationship. It seems a little fast."

I look at her, and she's looking down, away from the camera. "She is different," I say, truthfully, and she glances at me then, eyes widened.

"Riley, you seem like a smart girl. A rockstar? Really?" I glare at him, irritated, then I glance at Riley in an attempt to calm myself, and she's frowning. I see the same irritation in her expression.

Brock continues. "Is it the thrill of the lifestyle? And what exactly were you doing in his room when he walked in that night?"

Goddamn wanna be reporter. She is supposed to be off-limits!

I start to open my mouth to say that this interview is fucking over, when she speaks up. There is absolutely no sign of all that tension and nervousness in her tone. She is the one who reaches for my hand now.

"There was nothing to it. I'm a friend of the family from out of town, and I was staying over before the lock-down. And I don't see how what he does for a living and my decision to be with him, correlates with how smart I am." I shift on my seat and smile, wondering where the hell all that confidence came from.

He now glares at her as if he doesn't know what to ask next. At first, I don't know if he looks unimpressed or if her answer pissed him off. But either way, I fucking love it. His next question, answers my unspoken one.

His gaze stays on Riley as he asks, "Levi, how many have there been before Riley?" She flinches, pulling her hand away and I wonder if it is because of him using her real name, or the question itself.

"Definitely not as many as me!" Max says as he shows up, and I feel myself relax a little. Out of all of us, Max interviews best. He manages these guys better than anyone I know. "Come on. Get up," Max orders me. "It's my turn to interview." He pauses and bows in front of Riley, "Sleeping Beauty. It's a pleasure," he says as I stand up and give Max the chair. Then I extend my hand to her. She hesitantly takes it and I lead her away as

Bentley sits on the other chair, and they take over the interview.

Riley and I walk toward the bar, where Krissy is sitting, holding her phone up. "Shit. I'm sorry, Riley," I say. "I didn't think he would be that much of a dick."

She abruptly stops walking and I look at her. She has this terrified look in her eyes, and I know when she gaps for air, this is the beginning of another panic attack. Out of the corner of my eyes, I see Brock looking in our direction and moving to reach for his phone.

Without thinking, I move my hand toward her, like I did the first time she had a panic attack. Only this time, I rest my hand on the back of her neck, lean in, and kiss her.

Her arms go around me and I can feel the tension leave her body as she kisses me back.

With one kiss, she makes me forget where we are, or that there are cameras around.

When I pull away, her eyes are still closed. I lean back in and kiss her again, until she is ready to let go, and when she does, she looks dazed. Fuck. I probably do too.

"Hey! Look at this," Krissy says excitedly as she practically sticks the phone in our faces. Riley shakes her head and looks the other way, but I watch what she posted, and the way she focused on how I was looking at Riley, Riley's shyness during the interview, the close-up on our hands, gripping tightly for support, and then... the kiss. I know right away how this will turn out, which is only confirmed by the comments.

"That reporter is a dick."

"Who does he work for?"

"Don't worry, Riley. People do change, and I'm glad Levi changed for you."

The comments go on and on. "You're a genius," I tell Krissy, who curtsies. "I'm serious. The way you shot these… you told a whole story through a different lens."

"The way he looks at her," she titled the post, and I realize that she started a sort of exclusive news page for us.

"You, unlike that guy, have a real career in journalism," I tell her truthfully, and she gives me this huge proud smile. I hand her my phone. "You can share that through my Instagram."

Then, I look at Riley, and realize how angry she looks.

11

RILEY

"WHAT'S WRONG?" He asks, trying to reach for my hand, but I pull away, pretending to fix my hair.

"Nothing. This is just... too much," I say, looking around, avoiding eye contact. "I'm going back to the apartment."

"Okay," he says. "I have to get down there too. I have something for you," he says, excitement in his voice.

I really do hate surprises. And those words coming from someone who, according to the tabloids, has a history of doing crazy things, scare me. I sigh and look into his eyes then. "I've had enough surprises for a lifetime, Levi." The hint of a smile that was there vanishes. He looks heartbroken. And I feel like a jerk. I hear Krissy's phone ding over and over again. She has this huge smile on her face. We could leave right now and she wouldn't notice.

Feeling tired and defeated, I start to walk toward the

elevator with him. I can't wait to get off Bentley's shirt, because if I pick one more dog hair off it, I'm going to break. That's how much I miss my dog, and home.

Levi looks back toward the guys being interviewed and waves a quick goodbye in their direction.

The short elevator ride is the longest of my life. I keep catching myself glancing at his lips and replaying that kiss over and over again. When he looks at me, I quickly look away. And he looks amused too. Who knows… I probably look like one of his groupies crushing on him. *'I don't need this right now. I don't.'* I tell myself as I try to focus on a random spot on the floor.

We get to the apartment door, and I realize that Levi has this huge smile on his face.

"Let me," he says as he reaches for the door. Then he steps aside and I walk in. I gape as my dog, Wilson, charges in my direction.

"Wilson!" I say as I kneel down on the floor. "How?" I ask, looking at Marcia, as Wilson happily wags his tail and licks my face. "I missed you too!" I tell him. I then look at Marcia waiting for a reply and she nods over toward Levi.

"The boarding place called," he says, both hands in his pockets, and a smile on his face. "They're shutting down so we had to pick him up by 5 or they would have sent him to a shelter."

"But –" I start to say, confused, as I pet Wilson.

"Bentley used the private plane to go get him."

Tears well up in my eyes. Damnit. I want to be mad at him, but how can I now?

He kneels down next to me and gives Wilson a belly rub, and I look over at him. "Thank you," I say. "This means a lot," I start to cry – happy tears. Damn it. "Wilson is a rescue dog," I explain. "We adopted him from the shelter when he was about 3 years old. He had been there for over a year, and the thought of –" Levi cuts me off, pulling me into a side hug as I still rub Wilson's belly.

It should be illegal to give hugs as warm and comforting as this. This isn't fair. And I understand why people seem to let him get away with murder.

I look over at Marcia and she's watching him with such love in her expression. "But what about your mom?" I ask, looking up at him. "Can she even have pets here?"

He chuckles, moving his hand to my waist and giving me a small tug as he pulls me closer. "Yeah, Bentley's dad owns the building. He is cool. He loves pets. And Marcia offered to take in Wilson if mom bitches about it."

"Mr. Levi!" Marcia warns.

"Sorry. Sorry," he pulls away, raising his hands up. "If mom complains about it. But honestly, she'll do anything for her students. It'll be fine."

"Mr. Levi," Marcia says in a softer tone. "Speaking of your mom… she asked you to call her."

"Okay," he says, standing up. Wilson looks at him as if offended that he's no longer getting all the attention. "I guess I better go get this over with."

I stand up and go toward the couch with Wilson following me. I sit down, Marcia comes to sit next to me, and Wilson stands in front of me, resting his chin on my lap.

"Is he always like this?" I ask Marcia, looking toward the bedroom where he's staying. From the distance, I can see him sitting on the bed, his head lowered as if he's being chastised for something, and I wonder if it is because of Wilson being here.

"What do you mean?" She asks, and without taking my gaze off him, I say, "Impulsive. Irresponsible." I look at Marcia then, "I mean, I really, really appreciate him bringing Wilson here, but I could've had Krissy's parents pick him up."

She chuckles. "His heart is always in the right place. His head… not so much. But yes, he has always been like that. He can do something that makes you upset, and then turns around and makes this grand gesture that somehow makes it all okay. The funny thing is that he doesn't do the grand gestures to get out of trouble. He just randomly goes for it without thinking at all, honestly," she laughs. "And things have a way of working out."

He comes out of the room then, looking distraught, and my first thought is that his mom saw the video or wants Wilson gone, and I just know she's going to ask me to leave.

He leans against the wall and runs his fingers through his hair. "Mom has to drive from Georgia to Texas to pick-up dad. His program is shutting down because of the virus and she doesn't want him flying while this is going on," he says. "She said things are getting a little crazy out there with the numbers going up. They'll be gone for at least a week because of the drive and him packing up. Maybe more if dad has to quarantine for 2 weeks."

I give him a confused look. "But you have a private plane. Why is she driving for that long?" I ask.

He chuckles. "World crises or not, mother doesn't want anything to do with things that come from my life of debauchery and sins and all that," he rolls his eyes.

He looks at Wilson who is full on wagging his tail.

"Shit. I forgot about his food bowls, bed, and toys. I'll ask Bentley to go and –"

Marcia cuts him off. "It's fine. We can use bowls from the kitchen. I'll bring the rest tomorrow. And he can sleep on your bed tonight," she smiles at him.

"Okay, then. I'm going to crash. It's been the longest day of my life."

"Goodnight," I tell him, "and thank you."

He looks at me – his hazel green eyes piercing through me as a smile plays on his lips. "You're welcome, sleeping beauty. Goodnight."

'Why was I holding my breath through that?' I sigh

The moment I hear his door close, Krissy barges in through the front door.

"Come on. Girl talk!" She says as she motions to our bedroom. She then pauses and tilts her head. "Wilson?"

12

RILEY

We say goodnight to Marcia and go to the room, Wilson following.

I close the door behind me, take off Bentley's shirt and put it on the chair, wishing it was Levi's. *'Damnit,'* I think to myself as I sit on the bed where Wilson has already made himself comfortable, laying his head on my lap so I can pet him. I look at Krissy, ready for whatever she has to say.

"Okay, first," Krissy says as she paces back and forth. "Bentley is hot! Like, the whole package! You should've seen how he handled that Brock guy."

I roll my eyes at her.

"Second," she stops and looks at me. "THAT KISS between you and Levi. Holy hell, Riley! I wasn't even the one being kissed and I was getting hot."

I stop petting Wilson. I can feel my face getting warm,

tears springing to my eyes as I feel the anger building up again.

My phone rings and I see that it is Aunt Lilly; I answer right away as Krissy flops down next to me.

"Aunt Lilly. Is everything okay?"

"Yes," she says with a smile, but she looks exhausted.

"Where is mom?" I ask.

"She's out getting groceries."

"Oh. Okay." I say, but I notice this look in her eyes. She's up to something for sure.

"Do you want to know what I'm doing?" She asks coyly.

"Sure?"

"Well, I'm just over here, browsing my favorite websites for that good ol' gossip, and staring at a picture of my favorite niece being kissed by a rockstar." She says cheerfully, and I cover my face with my free hand as I shake my head. Krissy chuckles.

"Hi Krissy," Aunt Lilly says, waving at her.

Krissy leans closer to me, so Aunt Lilly can see her. "That was a hell of a kiss, wasn't it?"

I elbow Krissy on the arm. "Mom hasn't seen it, has she?" I ask, looking at Aunt Lilly again. My face is red.

"Nah. You know she won't waste time looking at those things," she says with a smile. "Tell me all about it!"

"Yeah, tell us ALL about it!" Krissy says next to me and I give her a side glare.

"There is really nothing to tell."

I explain to Aunt Lilly the whole social media and fake dating plan.

"That was it," I continue, getting frustrated again. "My very first kiss was a lie." I think about how long I'd waited for it. How I imagined it would've been with someone I had been on a date or two with before. And it would be romantic, sweet, and private - all of that gone.

"Oh, honey," Aunt Lilly says with a frown. Her tone softer. "This whole fake dating to get rid of the attention in a few days… horrible idea. Not just because that is not you, but you've just become the favorite 'it' couple after that interview. Even the ladies who want Levi, while jealous they still genuinely like you. I have yet to see one ugly comment, which is shocking, to be honest. Also, there is no way in hell that kiss was fake… or a lie." She pauses, studying my reaction, but I just look down. "Not to sound creepy, but I watched the video too. Riley –" she says, and I look up at her. "The way that boy looked at you – that was raw, and very real."

'No Aunt Lilly.' I think to myself. *'That is how I felt. It felt real. Too real. The kind of kiss that gave me butterflies. There is no way he felt the same. And I wish I hadn't either, because this will only end with me getting hurt.'*

"Which brings us to our next topic," Aunt Lilly says in a cheerful mood. "Safe sex."

"Please don't!" I beg her.

"Okay, fine," she says and I relax. A little. "But can you do something for me? You can think of it as a wish from my bucket list."

I raise an eyebrow at her. "That sounds a lot like emotional blackmail, Aunt Lilly."

She leans her head back, bursting into laughter. "You're not wrong, but I'm good with that."

"What?" I ask, afraid of the answer.

She grins. "I want Krissy to have full command over –" Krissy sits up straighter – excitement already radiating off her, "… three actions or decisions you make within the next month. Whatever she tells you to do. You have to do it. No questions asked."

"Yes!" Krissy stands up on the bed and jumps up and down. "This is the best thing ever!"

"No, it's not," I say as I look up at her.

"I hear the door," Aunt Lilly says in a whisper as she looks to the side. "Please, Ry. Do it for me. And be safe. Use condoms." I hide my face behind my hand again. "Make good choices. Have fun, but not too much fun," she says in a rushed tone. "I think that covers everything. Love you."

"Who are you talking to?" I hear mom's distant voice.

"Just an old friend from back home. Dating a celebrity. Fun, right?" she says as she hangs up the phone.

"Ugh," I growl.

"Is that why you were mad? Krissy asks as she sits back down. "The first kiss thing? Because, that really looked like some kiss."

Krissy reaches for her phone. "Wanna watch the video?"

I flinch. "No!" I yelp, making Wilson get up. "I don't want to see any of it," I sigh and lay down. "It's bad enough I'm crushing on him and I don't want to! I don't have time for that, and he – he is – well, you heard that guy. Who knows how many women he has been with."

"Soooo," Krissy says playfully. "You are crushing on him."

I sigh. “Is that the only thing you heard?” I ask.

“It’s the only thing that matters,” she grins.

13

(DAY 3)

LEVI

"I WAKE up to someone licking my face. A very slobbery someone. I make an attempt to open my eyes just enough to see Wilson, staring at me from the side of the bed. I move over. "Come on, boy," I say as I tap on the bed and Wilson hops up and lays down.

My eyes barely close again when I hear her. "Wilson! Where are you?" Riley whispers, and I'm awake again. Sort of.

"What time is it?" I ask Wilson as though he can answer. I roll over and grab my phone from the top of the other pillow. It's six thirty in the freaking morning. I roll back over.

"Wilson!" She says again. Closer this time. I hear him wag his tail on the bed, but he makes no attempt to move.

"Over here," I say sleepily.

"What are you doing there?" She whispers and I rub my eyes, trying to wake up. She is now by my door.

"Come on," she taps on her bare legs. "You're going to make me late!"

Okay, that gets my attention. I sit up. A lot more awake now. And holy fuck, she looks hot. I quickly grab a pillow and put it over my lap. Her hair is down, messy, and she's wearing one of our band's t-shirts. I'm thinking it's one of the ones from my drawer because it looks big on her and all I can think is... she's wearing one of my shirts, as I wonder what she has on underneath it. I adjust the pillow on my lap, without taking my eyes off her. And now that she catches me eyeing her, she reaches for the hem of the shirt and does a poor attempt at tugging it down, which makes me grin.

"It's six thirty. In the morning. And there is a lockdown. What are you late for? And is that what you are wearing? Because if it is, I am going too." I raise a brow at her. Wilson gets comfortable, lowering his head on the other pillow and closes his eyes.

She rolls her eyes at me. "Last I checked, you can't go anywhere. You know... house arrest and all," she grins and that takes me completely off-guard.

"Ouch," I say, putting my hands over my heart.

"I practice at seven," she says. "Every day."

"Okay, so you got 30 minutes."

"But I have to walk Wilson and make breakfast, and –"

I may not understand a lot, but I know what it's like to not have that routine of doing something you love, and that is what she's going through right now.

I start to get up, ignoring Wilson's protest when he glares at me like he's annoyed. "I feel you, buddy," I say as I reach for a shirt from the nightstand.

"What are you doing?" She asks. "I'll get him out of your hair. You should go back to sleep."

I yawn and I pull the shirt over my head. "I will. Later," I tell her. "Go get ready. I'll walk Wilson and make breakfast."

She tilts her head.

"Go on. I got this. I'll take Wilson up to the garden then I'll make you the best breakfast you've ever had."

"Do you always make things seem so easy?" She asks me.

"Yes. Now go!"

She looks from me to Wilson who is still passed out on my bed, and leaves the room as I watch her walk away.

Fifteen minutes later, Wilson and I get back to the apartment. Yeah, she's gonna be late. I look through my missed calls and messages. I see that I have six, seven… eleven missed calls from Lucifer. I ignore them, tossing the phone on the couch. Then I go over to the kitchen and open the fridge.

"How do you like your eggs?" I ask as she comes out of the room, wearing a tank top, yoga pants, and her hair in a perfect bun.

She pauses and gives me this look like I just asked her something crazy. "Are you telling me I can ask for eggs cooked in whatever way I want, and you can actually cook it?" She asks as she steps into the kitchen area and leans against the counter, watching me.

"Wow," I say as I grab eggs, cheese, mushrooms, tomatoes… stacking them up my arm as I grab each. Then I kick the fridge door closed and put everything on the counter, next to where she's standing.

She watches my every move, brows drawn together.

"You're totally stereotyping me right now," I say, faking being offended. "You don't think the hot rockstar can cook –"

She quickly cuts me off, looking horrified. "I didn't say that. I –"

I grin. "You agree that I'm hot."

She rolls her eyes at me. "Scrambled is fine," she says.

"Nah. Too easy." I reach for the drawer next to her, brushing my arm against her waist as I do. When I pull back, I put my arms on each side of her, pinning her against the counter. "How about I surprise you," I say with a wink.

"You don't know what I like," she retorts, her voice breaking. The sports bra makes it easy for me to notice how fast her chest rises and lowers. Her breathing quickens. I want to kiss her again. Right here. Right now. But I decide to give her space. The next move is all hers.

"Omelet with mushrooms, ham, cheese, avocado, and tomatoes?" I ask and she licks her lips, and there are parts of me awake that have no business being awake at the moment. Again.

She clears her throat. "Yes, please." She says as she ducks down under my arm and walks toward the door to feed Wilson.

Krissy comes out of the room then, already dressed.

"You too?" I ask and she gives me a confused and sleepy look. "Is my mom running a dance studio or a bootcamp?" I ask as I start to cook the ham and mushrooms.

"Both," Krissy says in a grumpy mood as she plops down on the chair. They sit quietly as I cook. Krissy's probably too sleepy to talk, and Riley is playing with Wilson.

When the food is done, I grab two plates and hand one to Riley. "Here, you can have mine," I tell Krissy, handing her the other plate. "Come on, Wilson," I say. "Ready to go back to bed?"

Before I go, I lean down toward Riley, grab her fork, and take a bite of her food, then I hand her the fork back as she gapes at me. "Enjoy," I say with a wink, before I go toward my room, with Wilson following me.

14

LEVI

It's a little after two in the afternoon when I roll out of bed and get up. I woke up to lyrics stuck in my head. Something that hasn't happened in a long ass time. I open my desk drawer, grab an old notepad, a pen, sit on the bed, and start to scribble it down.

How many times you've talked me back from the edge
Can we start over, begin again
I swear this until my last breath
Give me a chance, I'll love you til the end

When my phone rings, I grab it from my bed and see Sullivan's name. I roll my eyes and let it go to voicemail. Then I see another three missed calls.

He calls again.

"What?" I answer in an annoyed tone.

"Well, about fucking time." He pauses. "Since when do we give free interviews?" He snarls.

I take a deep breath, contemplating whether I should just hang up on him. I throw the notepad and pen to the side, because if there is one thing that kills my creativity, it's talking to management – Lucifer in particular.

"It was one interview. I think we'll survive."

"Yeah. Freebies are not part of the contract. We're going to auction off a meet and greet with the band to be hosted over there – to make up for the money we missed out on." The line goes silent for a moment and when I don't say anything, he goes on. "By the way, what's the deal with the girl?" He asks.

"She." I pause. "Is none of your business."

"On the contrary. You know what your fans really love? Available rockstars. Even this auction could be hindered by you trying to play house, so make it. go. away."

"Fucker." I say under my breath, pulling the phone away. I'll just ignore him as always. I put him on speaker, throw the phone on the bed, and start playing one of our old songs.

"Are you playing your guitar while I am talking to you?"

"No way," I say in a calm tone. "I wouldn't dare. It's the radio. Acoustic version." *'Dumbass,'* I leave that last part unspoken as I wonder if he would even be able to tell the difference.

Aaaand he hangs up.

I chuckle.

. . .

It's not until my stomach growls that I stand up, put my phone on silent, and go to the kitchen. Grabbing a can of coke and a lasagna dish that Marcia left behind, I turn to head to the table. I'm so hungry, I don't even care that it's cold.

"Oh. Hey." I say as I turn to find Krissy laying down on the couch watching TV with Wilson. I was so irritated by Lucifer, I zoned out while in the kitchen.

"Hey," she says back. Not sounding quite like her cheerful self.

"What are you watching? It can't be good with that expression. Did the bachelor pick the wrong chick or something?"

That gets a laugh out of her. "Probably, but that's not it."

"What's going on?" I pause and take a bite of the lasagna.

"Nothing," she says, looking back at the TV.

"Where is Riley?" I ask.

"Practicing."

"Still?!" I say with a mouthful.

"Well, she took a break earlier, but she needs the alone time though. Trust me. I've known her since we were little and dancing… alone… grounds her in a way. It kinda makes reality disappear for a little while."

No longer feeling hungry, I put the dish on the counter and head to join Krissy, holding my drink. I sit down next to her and look at the TV.

"I have a feeling you wouldn't be leaving dishes around if your mom was here," she says, still not sounding like herself.

"Good thing she isn't here." I nudge her shoulder. "Don't worry, I'll get it in a bit so Marcia won't have to." I grab the remote and am about to change the channel when I realize she's watching the news about the virus.

"You know this is just the media blowing things out of proportion, right? It's no worse than the flu."

"Yeah, you're wrong there," she says, then faces the TV again. "The fact that hospitals have to turn people away and morgues are full… It's far worse than you think."

"Things will get better though," I try to reassure her. I put on a music channel.

"Much better," I say as I lean my head back and turn to the side to look at her. "So… Riley. What's going on with her?"

Krissy sighs. "She was watching the news earlier. She's just worried. It looks like this mess is going to be longer than 14 days... Plus her aunt is in Thailand with her mom. Her aunt is high risk."

"Oh."

She continues. "I guess reality just really hit when we went out to take Wilson for a walk after lunch. The streets were empty. The few people we did see were apart from one another and wearing masks. It just sucks."

"It's temporary," I remind her. "Plus, you get to hangout with me, and sometimes the guys because of it all. It can't be that bad, right?"

"I guess not," she says with a laugh.

"Alright," I pull my phone out of my jeans pocket. "We're going to kick quarantine's ass."

"What are you doing?" She asks as I start typing on my phone.

"Making a list. Our very own Quarantine Survival Guide."

She watches me curiously as she drinks a can of coke while I finish typing, and then I hand her the phone.

Tonight… Karaoke night with the guys. Tomorrow… Movie night… the list goes on… game night, rooftop camping, and then Krissy spits out her drink as she reads the next one.

"Double date?" Krissy practically jolts forward. "Care to explain?" She asks.

"Sure. You're going on a rooftop date with Bentley. Me with Riley."

She squints her eyes at me. "Yeah. We'll see about that. Also, it's probably a horrible idea to have the guys come and go."

"You're right. Should they move in?" I ask jokingly and she rolls her eyes at me before she starts scrolling through her phone.

"We do need to have a serious talk though," she says, frowning and without looking up from her phone.

"About??" I ask curiously.

"Your intentions with my best friend, because this right here," she shoves the phone in my face, "is totally not going to help your case."

I have to do a double take to make sure it really says what I think it says.

"What. The. Fuck," I say before I get up and stomp toward my room.

15

RILEY

DANCING HAS ALWAYS BEEN my escape. When I'm dancing, I shut out the rest of the world. It's just me and the music. And my favorite part is that I don't think. I just let go, relax, and let the music guide my movements.

Today is a rare off-day, and I hate it. I couldn't focus this morning. My movements felt awkward – not in sync with the music – all because I couldn't stop thinking about him. And then, Krissy and I took Wilson for a walk.

I was afraid we'd run into paparazzi. Now I almost wish we had, because the alternative was far more unsettling. The streets were empty and quiet. There were a few people here and there – all distant from one another. A little girl who was maybe three or four wearing a mask that covered half of her face. There were no sounds of cars going by – impatiently honking their horns. No one chattering, no laughter – nothing. When I felt my heart starting to pound against my chest, I tried to take a deep breath, and all I could hear in my head was his voice. *"Close your eyes, Riley.... Deep breaths."* And just like that, I was fine.

Now that I'm back up on the apartment's rooftop, alone, I'm determined to center myself and focus, but I can't seem to just get back to it like I usually do. The walk was supposed to clear my head, but it only added to my stress, so I decide to explore the garden. I'm surprised when I walk past the small entrance and find three routes. I've never been past this point before. I choose the one in the middle and walk the short distance to the center where there are three sunbeds. The sun is out today, so I lay down on one of them and FaceTime mom.

Aunt Lilly cheerfully answers the phone. "Hey favorite niece." She looks a lot better today – not as tired as last time we spoke.

"Hi Aunt Lilly," I say with a smile. "How are things? Where is mom?"

"She is sleeping."

I smack my forehead. "Argh. I keep forgetting the time difference."

Aunt Lilly laughs. "It's fine. What are you doing? It looks like you are somewhere I would approve of. Show me around."

I put the phone up and do a full circle so she can see the surroundings.

"Definitely approve. It's just missing some music, and someone to sing it for you," she winks.

"Nah." I tell her. "He is trouble."

"Even better!" She grins.

"Aunt Lilly!"

"I'm serious, sweetheart. Just have some fun. Life goes by in a blink," she says with a frown, and my heart sinks. I blink back the tears.

"Hey! Don't you make that face!" She says in a soothing tone. "Well, I should get some sleep, sweetheart. I'll chat with you soon." She gives me a wicked smile. "In the meantime, I'll be checking out this rockstar's Instagram for more."

I just shake my head.

"Love you, Aunt Lilly."

"Love you, favorite niece. Tell Krissy I said hi."

After we hang-up, I close my eyes and end up falling asleep.

It's not until I hear two people arguing that I open my eyes and quietly walk toward the entrance.

LEVI

I storm into Carly's room and call Lucifer. Voicemail. Pacing back and forth, I hang-up. Call again. Voicemail. I repeat the process over and over a few more times before he answers.

"Well, now you know how that feels," he says, sounding annoyed.

I stop walking and start yelling into the phone. "You can't just go around auctioning off dates. Take it down," I demand.

"Look. I can't tell you what to do during said date, but I can definitely run the auction. Think of it as a meet and greet in a romantic setting. Have dinner. Take some pictures, and that is it."

"I'm on house arrest."

"Based on your interview, that rooftop is a pretty good place. Make it a group thing with the other guys, if that makes you feel better."

"There is a lockdown, you know?" I remind him.

"They will be tested."

This is pointless. Frustrated, I hang-up, grab my wallet and barge back in the living room where Krissy is still sitting down, looking at her phone.

"Busy?" I ask.

She shakes her head. "Just watching to see how pricey you guys get. One date for each of you – it's getting a bit crazy."

I let out a deep breath, open my wallet, pull out a credit card, and extend it to her.

She raises an eyebrow at me. "What do you want me to do with that?"

"Bid."

"On Bentley?" She asks with a grin.

I flop down on the couch next to her. "Just get me out of this, please. Whatever it takes."

She looks from me to the card I am holding. "You know… you could do this yourself and just add Riley's name as the winner."

I pause. "Please," I beg. "I can't personally bid on myself. That's just too fucking weird. And if the guys found out, I would never hear the end of it."

Krissy laughs and grabs the card. "Guys and their pride," she jokes. "You know… You're already past 10k."

"Shit. Seriously?" My eyes widen. "What about the other guys?"

Krissy rolls her eyes. "They're close, but not as much as you."

"Ha," I say, ready to text Bentley to brag about it when she reminds me that just means I'll be paying a lot of money.

"Limit?" She asks.

"No limit. Just get me out of it, please."

"Are you sure about this? I mean, this is just like a meet and greet, right? It's not like you have to sleep with the winner. Please tell me that is not what's happening here."

"No, but you said so yourself. That does not help my case."

She grins at that.

"You've proven yourself to me. I have your back and I will just talk to Riley about it."

I sigh. "Honestly," I pause. "I probably sound like such an ass, but I'm not even in the mood to spend time with anyone else. Just the thought of having to make small talk…" I shake my head.

"Okay, then," she says as she starts typing. Then she suddenly stops and looks up at me.

"We have a problem," she says.

I wave my hand up. "What now?"

She looks from me to her phone, and then back. "There is a disclaimer saying that bidders cannot be associated with the band in any way, including friends or family members."

"Well. Fuck."

16

RILEY

I TAKE a peek through the garden and see that it is actually just one person, arguing with someone on the phone. The man wearing a suit has his phone on speaker and he walks behind the bar looking for something. He slams the phone down on the counter and yells out every word as if the person on the call can't hear him. "Are you fucking kidding me? How can you find nothing on this girl?" His face is red from anger as he puts a glass bottle he found on the counter and opens it. "The girl wasn't even on social media before this for fucks sake. She has to be hiding something."

I take a step back, afraid to be seen now that I know he's talking about me. *'Who is this guy?'* I think to myself.

"I don't know what to tell you. There is no dirt. Nothing," the voice on the phone tells him.

The man makes a fist and slams it down on the counter, making me flinch. He is quiet for a moment.

"Okay. Plan B it is. If there is one thing about Levi," he almost spits out the name. "Is that he's predictable. He'll always love the obsessed love-sick groupies. He thinks he owes them the world for making him famous," he rolls his eyes, grabbing a cup from behind the counter and pouring the drink into it. Suddenly, his voice sounds higher and full of excitement. "That one-night stand turned stalker from last year..." His tone changes to something dark, making my stomach churn. "I don't care what it takes. Just make sure she wins. This dancer... Riley," he snarls, making me inch back, "is a problem, and that is the solution."

He chugs his drink and fills up the glass again.

"You know, people are responding well to this relationship." The guy on the phone tells him. "They like her. They like the mystery. They like them together."

He takes another drink then puts the glass down with such force I'm surprised it doesn't shatter. "This needs to end. Levi is bored. That's what this is all about. But we need it to end sooner rather than later. Yeah, people are all over it today. But they'll get bored and she's going to start costing us sales, which impacts my bank account."

"You do know they have talent, right? People do go see them because their music is great. Not just because they are single and fun."

The man grabs the phone, bringing it closer to his lips. "I hired you for PI work, not for advice on things you know nothing about. The single, fun, reckless vibe works for him. It's part of the appeal. And this is why I'm their manager and not you," he growls.

"So, that is their manager," I mumble under my breath.

I have a million questions running through my mind. *He wants this girl to win what?* I wonder.

Finally, he walks toward the elevator and presses the button, still holding up his phone, and then a familiar voice answers.

"Hello?"

"Hi Mrs. O'Connor," he says in a much calmer tone. "This is Sullivan." He pauses and sighs. "I think we need to talk. I'm a little concerned about Levi."

LEVI

I'm sitting down on the couch, texting the guys to come over tonight as I watch TV with Krissy. Wilson is plopped down in the middle, pawing at Krissy every time she stops petting him.

I text the group.

Me: Please, for the love of God, bring some pizza and junk food. As much as I love Marcia's cooking, I've had nothing but homemade food these past few days.

When I look up from my phone, I see Riley standing by the front door, watching me, but her expression seems off. Her cheeks look flushed. Wilson's tail is now wagging nonstop, but with Krissy petting him, he doesn't move.

"Everything okay?" I ask as I put the phone down on the coffee table.

"Yeah. Why?"

Krissy grabs the remote, turns the TV off and looks at Riley. "Because you look like you've seen a ghost," she says.

"Everything is okay," she stammers. "What are you two doing?"

Krissy chuckles. "Well, Levi here is being sold."

Riley raises an eyebrow at her.

"Way to make me feel cheap," I joke.

"OOOHHHH" Krissy laughs. "You're definitely not cheap. 18k as we speak."

"You're kidding!" I say, and Riley just looks back and forth between us. Confused. And I know this isn't going to win me any points with her. At all. I try to make it sound better than it actually is. "The label is doing a meet and greet auction," I say as I watch her for a reaction. But at the moment, I can't read her.

"You do that type of thing all the time, though, don't you?" She finally asks.

"Sort of," I say, standing up. I start to move toward her. My gaze fixed on hers. "Would that bother you?"

"Why would it?" She asks. Still standing rooted in the same spot. It's almost like she is standing there, calculating every move. Every word. "We're only fake dating. Besides, it's part of your job, right?" She asks as she bites her bottom lip.

I keep staring at her, and when I close the distance between us, I reach for her and lift her chin. I want her to be looking at me when I say my next words. "What if I don't want it to be fake?"

She steps back and shies away but there is no hint of a smile. Nothing. And she doesn't have to tell me this isn't happening. I can see it in her eyes; in her body language.

I stay put but give her a smile in an attempt to let her

know that this is okay. I'm a big boy. I can handle rejection. Shit. That is a lie. I fucking hate this feeling.

My phone ringing saves us from the awkward silence and pity that is undoubtedly coming my way. I turn around and walk over to the coffee table, grabbing my phone.

I can't help but roll my eyes before I answer it.

"Hey, mom," I answer in a serious tone, looking at Wilson as I pet him with my other hand.

"LEVI JAMESON!" She yells into my ear. I pull the phone away as I sigh and walk toward Carly's room.

17

RILEY

I STAND HERE, unable to move. *'What if I don't want it to be fake?'* His question plays over and over in my head. *'Why would he say that?'* There's no way he meant it. His manager was right. He's stuck at home and bored, and even if he wasn't, this would never work. We're too different, we – the front door opens and Bentley and Max along with another guy and a girl come barging into the apartment. Wilson, now wagging his tail at full speed, goes to check them out – specifically, checking out Bentley who is holding a few pizza boxes. The third guy and the girl are the only ones wearing masks and they stand back by the door. I wave a quick hello before I distance myself from all of them by walking toward the other side of the room where Krissy is sitting down. I sit next to her and instantly reach for my phone – my escape during awkward gatherings.

"OMG! Is that pizza I see, or am I dreaming?" Krissy

asks excitedly as she stands. "I thought restaurants were closed right now." Bentley smiles as he walks toward the kitchen. "Yep. Perks of knowing the restaurant's owner. And it was a special request from Levi. Where is he anyway?"

I glance up above my phone.

"On the phone with his mom," Krissy says.

"Ahhh. This is Kev and his friend, Ginny, by the way," Bentley points at the guy and girl standing by the front door. He puts the pizza boxes down, and I notice he's wearing another one of the band's t-shirts – only, this one is gray and says, *'Drummers are hotter.'* I let out a small laugh as I shake my head. We all say the awkward hellos and nice to meet you, and Krissy is already opening the top pizza and reaching for one. "I was starving!" She says before she takes a huge bite.

Bentley chuckles and moves toward her, reaching for a slice too. "I thought you tiny little ballerinas didn't eat stuff like that," he nudges her shoulder and Krissy rolls her eyes before she takes another bite. "We have drinks too," Bentley continues, pointing at Max, who I now notice is carrying a case of beer in one hand, and sodas in the other.

Wilson is having the time of his life with so many people around.

Feeling awkward just being here, and in desperate need to just be alone and process what happened earlier, I quietly make my way to the bedroom to change.

I close the door to block off the sound of their chattering and laughing. Instead of changing, I lay down on the bed.

'Okay, so obviously his manager wants the girl that he mentioned to win the auction.' I think to myself. A part of me feels like I should warn Levi. The other part thinks that maybe I shouldn't get in the middle. That it would just create problems between him and his manager, and that is the last thing I want. I contemplate that back and forth before deciding that Levi being who he is, and working in that madness for so long, can handle this. "It's not my business. I'll stay out of it," I tell myself. Besides, I have bigger problems to think about, like what the hell am I going to do when Mrs. O'Connor kicks me out for that kiss with Levi…

'What if I don't want it to be fake?'

Why, why does that keep sneaking up into my mind?

I text Aunt Lilly since she knows the whole fake dating thing.

Me: Can we talk? Alone.

She FaceTimes me right away.

"Hey, Aunt Lilly. Did I wake you?"

"Nah. Can't sleep again. What's going on?" She asks, and I feel bad for bugging her. She looks tired.

"I can call you in the morning if you want," I say.

"Not a chance, favorite niece. Whatcha got?"

"I have a problem," I say, looking down.

"What is it?" She asks in a concerned tone.

"I like him," I say in a whisper.

She chuckles. "I already knew that. What's the real problem?"

I sigh and look back up at her. "He made this comment about the whole fake dating thing… 'What if I don't want it to be fake?'"

"Riley," she says playfully. "This should be a good thing."

"No, it shouldn't!" I say, raising my voice, my brows knitted, "We're completely different in every imaginable way. His lifestyle, his personality… when things are back to normal, we'll be going in two completely different directions."

"Riley," she says, leaning forward. "I want you to listen to me carefully, okay?" I nod. "You don't have to choose. You can have fun and still do what you love. You can have it all. You just have to adapt to make it work."

Tears well up in my eyes.

"What is this really about, sweetheart?" She asks in a softer tone.

I start to sob. "I'm mad at myself for liking him."

"Why?"

"B-because I waited so long and then my first kiss was with someone who is just bored because he doesn't have random girls jumping at him all the time like he usually does."

"Where is this coming from, Riley? Because I really don't think that is true, sweetheart."

"I don't know," I tell her, wiping my eyes with the back of my hand.

"You want my advice?" She asks and I catch my breath. "Yeah."

"I think maybe you should quit this fake dating nonsense. Take a step back and get to know him. I have a gut feeling you may be surprised."

I tilt my head to the side. Maybe she's right, but I don't know if I want to find out. I swallow the lump in my throat. "I should go," I tell her. "Get some rest. I'll call you tomorrow. Love you," I say.

"Love you too, favorite niece." She grins.

Seconds go by before there is a knock on the door. I find it strange that Krissy would knock because she usually is the barge in type, but maybe she realized I needed the space. I do my best to not look like I'm a sobbing mess.

"C-Come in," I stammer.

The door slowly opens and Levi pokes his head in.

"Hey," he says.

I quickly sit up as he opens the door all the way.

"Hey. Your friends are here," I tell him, feeling stupid for mentioning it since we can hear them talking and laughing.

"Yeah, I'll get to them. Are you okay?"

"This is it, isn't it?" I say, as I pull the pillow onto my lap. "Your mom knows about the kiss and wants me out of here."

"Is that why you are upset?" he asks, concerned.

I don't reply, because I don't want to lie to him.

He shakes his head and laughs, but it's a nervous laughter. "Trust me, my mom would kick me out before she asks you to leave."

I give him a puzzled look.

"She wouldn't do that," I tell him.

"Oh. She definitely would," he says as he approaches the bookshelf.

"Why do you think that?" I ask.

He turns away from the bookshelf holding the CD with my favorite song to dance to as he looks at me.

"Because I gave up what she wanted me to do with my life, for what I wanted to do." He pauses and puts the CD down. "Well, enough of that sappy story. Come on," he says as he extends his hand to me. "We're going to the rooftop for pizza and games."

I hesitate and he nudges me. "Come on. Let's go before they eat all the pizza."

I take his hand then, but let go as soon as I stand. For a split second, I see the look of hurt in his eyes. "What did your mom say about it though? Was she mad?"

He raises an eyebrow at me, "How do you know that's what she called about anyway?"

LEVI

The moment I ask her how she knew, she looks down and starts to nervously crack her knuckles.

"Did she say something to you about it?" I ask, all the while thinking about what I had just heard. How I was her first kiss. Before, I couldn't stop staring at her lips because I wanted more. She's different in more ways than I anticipated. And now, I'm weirdly terrified of kissing her again, but even more terrified of not getting to.

"No, she didn't," she says, avoiding my gaze.

"Lucky guess?" I ask.

She bites on her bottom lip as if contemplating answering my question.

"I – I don't want to cause any problems by answering that."

I shrug. "You won't. I'm just curious."

"I heard your manager calling her," she says.

Huh. It seems that Lucifer still has the power to surprise me. "When? Where? Did he say anything to you?" I blurt out as I take a step toward her.

She moves back, putting more distance between us.

"On the rooftop earlier today. He didn't see me. I was hiding. Why was he there anyway?" She asks.

"That fucker. Sorry. I shouldn't cuss," I say and she lets out a chuckle. "The... hmmm.... The shithead..." that makes her smile. God, that smile! "He is Bentley's brother. His dad owns the building," I say, not remembering if I mentioned it before.

She's looking nervous again and avoiding my gaze.

"There is more, isn't there?" I ask, and I swear if he was the one that put it in her head that I'm just bored...

She nods. "But it's none of my business, really."

"Please?" I beg. "I like to be prepared when it comes to Lucifer's plotting."

She laughs. "Please tell me his name is not actually Lucifer."

I smile at her, unable to stop myself from reaching forward to move a lock of her hair back. I slowly pull away. Surprised that she doesn't step back this time. "His name is Grant Sullivan. But Lucifer just fits him better."

She shakes her head then sighs. "That auction that you were talking about. He – hmm – he told someone to make sure the winner is some girl who stalked you last year."

I take one loooong deep breath, remembering the rumors about her being a one-night stand. I grab my phone and start typing a message.

"What are you doing?" Riley asks in an alarmed tone. "I really didn't want to create any problems."

"Nothing," I say. "Just texting my favorite security guy to make sure he can work when that night comes. Everything will be fine. Trust me." I put my phone away when I'm done and look at her. "You're not in trouble with my mom, by the way. Me on the other hand," he laughs. "...but nothing new there. She's going to make sure Marcia is here more often, but that's because of me. Not you. She trusts you," I say.

"Okay," she says.

"Alright then," I look down for a split second, let out a breath and then look at her and extend my hand. "Hi. I'm Levi O'Connor."

She raises an eyebrow, giving me the expected confused look, but slowly grins as she puts her hand in mine.

"You and I are starting over," I tell her. "That guy in the tabloids. That's not the real me. I'm going to show you who I really am, and then I'm going to ask you out on a real date."

18

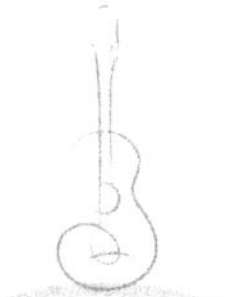

RILEY

LIFE outside of the studio was never a thing for me. Sure, there were the occasional sleepovers at Krissy's and birthday parties, but that was about it. Aunt Lilly always said I was the most unusual teen she had ever seen because while Krissy went out with the rest of the girls in class, I mostly stayed back. Boring, I know.

It is no surprise that my first instinct is to flee as I stand here on the rooftop, watching them turn the string lights on and move a few chairs from the bar around so we can sit down to eat. I end up sitting down next to Krissy. Bentley sits next to her, then Kev, Ginny, and Max – leaving a chair open for Levi next to me. Feeling awkward being the only one now wearing a mask, I take it off. I start to run the usual excuses through my head, *It's getting late... I'm not hungry... I need to wake up early tomorrow...* when out of the corner of my eye, I see Levi grab a guitar that was leaning against the wall and start to strum the chords as he walks toward us, and holy– "Need a napkin to wipe that drool," Krissy leans in and whispers, chuckling.

That is when I realized I was gaping. I close my mouth and glare at her.

"You never heard his music before, have you?" She asks and I shake my head, feeling guilty. "No. Especially not like this." I tilt my head to the side as I watch his every move. He is too focused on the guitar to look up; so for the first time, I feel like I can really take him in without the fear of getting caught. And he looks so happy. So confident. So ugh.... Yeah, he looks hot. "Something about what he's playing sounds familiar," I say, feeling Krissy's gaze on me.

"Just wait until he starts singing. You'll be needing that napkin for sure," she jokes and if on cue, he starts to sing as he closes the distance between us.

You opened my eyes
Showed me how to live
You took my hand
Told me there's so much more to give
I was a fool for not seeing
What was right in front of me
With you
Is where I'm supposed to be

I am speechless. I swallow the lump in my throat, trying to find the words, and I just can't. He's insanely talented, and I love the smile on his lips when he's doing what he loves.

"Wow. Wow. Wow!" Says Max as he leans back on the chair and claps. "Are you writing again? And why are we just now hearing this one?" He asks as Levi looks from me, to him.

Levi keeps playing as he sings, "Because it's not done," and he stops, tapping his hand on the guitar before he puts it down near the table and sits next to me.

"So what are we doing tonight?" Kev asks.

"Well, Krissy and I put together a quarantine survival list. Games tonight. Karaoke tomorrow –"

Bentley cuts him off. "Can't tomorrow. We have that label auction date night thing."

'Date?' I think to myself. I happen to look at Ginny then and I can see she doesn't look happy. Then I look at Levi and he's staring right back at me, his eyes widened like he did something wrong or didn't want me to know that.

"Meet and Greet," he quickly corrects Bentley.

"Yeah. That. Anyway… that's tomorrow."

"I thought they had to get tested first?" Levi says in an annoyed tone.

"Damn. How far are you planning to take that meet and greet," Max says in a playful tone before he takes a huge bite of his pizza.

"For the virus, dumbass," Levi says before he looks at me, as if searching for a reaction. I instinctively look away from him and my gaze lands on Max instead.

He shrugs. "Sorry, Sleeping Beauty," Max says. "I'll personally make sure he's on his best behavior."

I shake my head. I'm never going to escape that nickname.

Bentley bursts into laughter. "You can barely handle yourself. Let alone others."

"Well, Lucifer said the tests are handled," Kev says.

I scoff, "I wouldn't trust that even if he swore it on his mom's life." I clasp my hands over my mouth when I realize I said it out loud and they're all looking at me.

They chuckle. "She's not wrong," Levi reaches for my hand under the table. "We'll handle it," he says.

As Max opens another pizza box, I'm back to plotting my exit. Krissy leans into me. "I know that look," she whispers. "You have to stay. Your aunt said I get to make three decisions for you. This is the first. Stay and play whatever game we play."

"That's two decisions," I tell her.

She crosses her arms over her chest as she stares at me. "Fine. I will take it," she finally says. "Two decisions, but I feel like I'm being cheated."

"Uh-huh," I tell her as we each grab a slice of pizza.

"So, what game are we playing?" Krissy asks.

"The initiation game," Max says with a grin.

LEVI

"Fuck me," I whisper under my breath. Riley and Krissy are both looking at Max for more information when Bentley leans in and says in a low tone, "You know we got your back."

"Yeah," I whisper, leaning toward him. "But you can't control what they are gonna ask."

I give her hand a soft squeeze. "It's Never Have I Ever," Max explains. "You're new to us. We need to know things."

"Pass," Riley says nervously, and part of me relaxes a bit. I'm about to say we can do something else when Krissy interrupts, pointing at Riley. "No. You have to. You know the deal."

"Ugh," Riley rolls her eyes at Krissy and I watch the interaction curiously.

"Isn't there alcohol involved in this thing? Because if there is –" Riley says.

"You never played?" Max asks, full of excitement, which to be honest, makes this even more scary.

"Come with me," I say as I stand, and she follows my lead. I look back at Krissy. "You too."

We go behind the bar. "I'll explain our rules."

I look back at Bentley, "Did your dad ever order those flasks for us to sign so he can sell them?"

"Yep. Behind the bar. Why?"

"Because it is a fucking pandemic and I'm not drinking out of the same bottle as Max's sorry ass. And neither are they," I nod toward Riley and Krissy.

"Yeah, I'm totally not doing that either," Bentley laughs, and so do Kev and Ginny. Max is frowning and looking, well… confused. When he puts two and two together, his expression relaxes. "Whatever," he says.

"Usual drinks?" I ask and they all nod.

I let go of Riley's hand to reach for the box under the

counter and grab the black flasks with our band's name on it.

"So, the game is simple," I start. "You say something you have never done. Everyone who has done that, drinks."

"I'm not drinking," Riley tells Krissy, sounding defensive. "And you can't use the third to get me to do it," she crosses her arms over her chest.

I put the flasks on the counter and look at them. "Just so I know I haven't gone crazy... you are talking in codes right now, right?"

At first, I don't know if they even hear me. They're in some kind of staring contest.

"I'm starting to question your sanity regardless of the answer to this question," Riley says and that... I'm not sure where that comment came from, but it makes me smile. There are rare moments when it feels like she lets a bit of her true self come out. The more carefree, not having the weight of the world on her shoulders type moments. That was one of them.

I grab a bottle of coke that the guys brought in and start to pour it into the flasks.

"Max and Bentley are the only drinkers here," I explain as they watch me. "The flasks make it easier to hide that. The perks of a pandemic," I shrug. "So you basically have to pretend that you're drinking and act like a fool for Max's sake. Bentley doesn't care. He knows we will have water or soda. But after a while," he scoffs. "Max will be too drunk to notice. Also be prepared, because the more Max drinks, the worse the questions get. The only downside for the rest of us not drinking is that we'll remember the answers tomorrow," I wink at Riley.

"And if I want to drink?" Krissy asks as she raises an eyebrow at me.

"I will say hell no, because for one thing, Marcia is stopping by tonight. And there is also the little problem with you being underage."

She shrugs, grabs her flask and heads to the table. Riley stays exactly where she is. I reach for the flasks to head to the table when I feel her hand on my wrist. I look over at her.

"Everything okay, Sleeping Beauty?" I give her a reassuring smile.

She shakes her head nervously.

"I'm the wrong person to play this," she says in a low tone.

"How come?" I ask, staying right where I am, because the last thing I want right now is for her to stop touching me.

"Because I'm horrible at pretending. And I feel like I have never done anything." She looks embarrassed.

"Yeah, you have," I say with a crooked smile. She watches me curiously. "You've kissed a rockstar."

19

LEVI

I WAS NOT BLINDED to her lifestyle. If anything, her dedication to doing what she loves is one of the things I admire about her, besides the fact that she is insanely beautiful and she doesn't even realize it. With my mom being a teacher, I grew up surrounded by dancers. I know the dedication that it takes; yet I heard of girls getting in trouble for skipping classes, sneaking out and doing things like all teenagers do. Hell, my sister quit dancing because she was through with it all. Of course, it didn't help that mom was extra hard on her. Still, as I sit here next to Riley, I can't help but feel heartbroken. She definitely wasn't kidding. Never been camping… never faked being sick… never been on a boat… never skipped school… never been to a concert! I was a little offended by that one. The worst part is that she's truly embarrassed for not having done these things. She feels like she's missing out, but she still chooses dance. She doesn't realize she doesn't have to choose, and I'm going to show her that.

I give Bentley, Ginny and Kev a look begging for help here. I skip Krissy because this whole time, she has already been trying to cater what she says to help Riley feel included. And Max – well, he is Max. He is already not thinking straight. Bentley on the other hand – he knows when to stop.

"Never have I ever had a video go viral," Ginny says with a smile.

'Thank you!' I mouth to her.

I bump Riley with my shoulder and she laughs before she takes a drink of her coke.

"Never have I ever... secretly read someone's messages," Bentley says.

"Liar," I call out. We all get a good laugh at that. We all drink. Him included.

"Never have I ever kissed a musician," Kev says, and Riley and Ginny are the only one who drink. Although Ginny hesitated. But... three in a row for Riley. She looks more relaxed. I feel more relaxed.

Max's turn comes around. "Finally!" He says, looking bored. "I never had a one-night stand." His speech slurs.

'Fucker,' I think to myself. I swear, he always goes back for seconds just so he can pull this card when we play.

I drink. Bentley drinks. And Riley shifts in her seat and won't meet my eyes.

"Never have I ever danced in the rain," I say.

"Boohoo," Max taunts me. "Asshole," I say.

Riley, Krissy and Ginny all drink. "Huh. It must be a

girl thing, which also explains why Levi brought it up," Max says, aaaaand he should be cut off soon.

"Never have I ever played strip poker," Krissy says and Max cracks up. Riley and Ginny are the only ones who don't drink.

'Shit. At what point do I start lying?' I think to myself.

"Never have I ever dressed up as the easter bunny, cupid, or Santa Claus to visit children's hospitals during a holiday."

Thank God for Bentley.

I drink and Riley looks over at me, looking surprised.

"You do that?" She asks.

"Every single holiday. No matter where we are touring," Bentley answers for me, and I nod. "I don't like to brag. It's a me thing. It doesn't need to be all over the news."

Her breath catches as she looks at me, until Max interrupts. "Never have I ever called a partner by the wrong name," I turn to glare at him and I realize he has his phone up, facing us.

"What are you –?"

Bentley cuts me off, snatching the phone from Max's hand and stopping whatever he was doing.

"What?" Max asks, confused. His speech slurred. "Don't get all pissed off. I'm doing you a favor. Lucifer texted me and said we were all late streaming. So I got everyone covered."

"Can I hit him?" Kev asks.

"Just – delete the video," I snap, looking at Bentley. I'm already standing up and going for the phone so I can delete it myself if he doesn't.

"You know that we can't," Bentley says quietly, moving the phone back so I can't reach it.

"What's going on?" Max stands next to me and pokes a finger at my chest. It takes everything I have not to shove him back right now. He goes on. "You never cared what ended up on social media or the tabloids or what people said." He pauses and looks at Riley. "Maybe Lucifer has a point. Sleeping beauty is bad for business."

RILEY

'Great! I'm the cliche that breaks up the band and I'm not even actually dating the guy,' I think to myself as I quietly stand up. The last thing I want to do is be here right now. While they're arguing back and forth about me, Lucifer, and their contract when it comes to deleting videos, I step away and try to get out of here, hoping no one notices me leaving. I take a few steps away before Krissy walks up to me, snakes her arm through mine and leads me to the elevator.

"I hate this," I whisper to her, tears welling up in my eyes as we wait for the elevator.

"Yeah, I know," she says. "That is why you froze when he said he didn't want the dating to be fake, isn't it? You didn't want to cause trouble?" She asks.

"Among many other reasons," I say truthfully.

When the elevator door opens, two cops stand in there, towering over us. They are both maybe in their forties, both wearing masks, and both give us stern looks.

"Is Levi Jameson O'Connor here?" The tallest of the two cops asks with a heavy new yorker accent.

I feel like my heart stops beating. A million thoughts race through my mind. He hasn't done anything. He's been in the apartment like he's supposed to.

"Y-yes," Krissy stutters.

They start to walk out, and we are both frozen in place. "You two – come with me." His partner says in a surprisingly soothing tone that doesn't cause me to have a panic attack right now, and I assume that if they ever do the whole good cop - bad cop thing, he's the nice one.

"What is this about?" Krissy asks, her voice sounding more composed, while I am still in shock. Without saying a word, the cops lead us toward the guys, who are still arguing as Ginny tries to get their attention.

The nice cop faces Krissy. "We received reports of underage drinking," he says as the guys turn around, and everyone goes quiet.

20

(DAY 4)

RILEY

"NEVER HAVE I ever been questioned by a cop. Well, scratch that off the list," I say as I grab my folded clothes off the top of the dresser and start to throw them into the open suitcase on the bed. "Never have I ever taken a breathalyzer. There goes another one."

"Are we really doing this?" Krissy asks me while sitting on the bed, watching my every move. "We got cleared right away. No one got in trouble. If anything, the cops were surprised there wasn't anything illegal happening."

I twirl around and glare at her. "Yes, I'm sure." I say before I continue packing. I'm an organized person, but at the moment, I don't even care. I continue throwing clothes in there. "You saw it on the news this morning. They are extending the lockdown," I tell her. "There is no point in staying," I say and it's not until I hold my ballet shoes in my hands that I stop packing and just stare at them. This could be it. The end of it all. And I have no clue what to do with the rest of my life.

"Okay," she says. "But I think we should tell Levi before I call my parents. You know once I tell them there is no going back. They're already freaking out about this virus and want me home."

I look up from my shoes to her. "You mean we should call Mrs. O'Connor and tell her," I correct Krissy. I don't wait for her reaction before I slowly place my shoes in the suitcase and close my eyes for a split second without letting go of my hold on it. "Levi has nothing to do with this," I pause before I look back at her. "Or is this the third wish because you think if I see him - or tell him - I'll change my mind?" I snap.

Krissy just stares at me with her mouth hanging open.

I sigh, sitting down on the bed next to her. "Ugh. I'm sorry Krissy. I didn't mean to take this out on you. It's just –"

"Frustrating," she says. "I know. But I think Mrs. O'Connor may have a lot on her plate right now. I mean, we haven't heard directly from her in a while; surely Levi talks to her on a daily basis. I think he can decide on the best time to tell her and then, we'll go from there."

"Okay. I'll tell him."

I march out of the bedroom to get this done and over with, because I'm afraid that if I wait to talk to him, I'll give in and stay, just because – just because that means being around him. *Ugh. I do not want this.*

I come to an abrupt stop when I see him sitting on the

couch, leaning forward. His head down, his shoulders moving up and down as if he's crying.

My heart skips a beat. "Levi?" I say in a low tone.

Nothing.

I walk closer.

"Levi."

Still nothing, but I can hear him sniffling.

I close the distance between us, sit on the couch next to him and put a hand on his shoulder.

"Levi, is everything okay?" I ask, and without looking up at me, he turns and pulls me into a hug. And just like that, the anger I felt a second ago vanishes. My arms instantly go around him.

"What happened?" I ask.

He doesn't pull away. "Marcia. She-she is in the hospital," he says against my neck. "Her husband has the virus, but didn't know at first." I try to pull away to look at him, but he just pulls me back in. A million things run through my mind. *Is she okay? Do we have it?*

When he finally pulls away, his eyes are red. He slips his hand into mine and he stares at our hands as he says, "Her husband thought he just had a cold and cough last week. She was hospitalized last night. That's why she didn't show. She has asthma so it doesn't look good. Her husband was the one who called me. He's freaking out and blaming himself," He pauses, still staring at our hands. "They aren't letting anyone but patients in the hospital. She is all alone." He looks up at me then. "I've been calling to try to move her to a private room. See if maybe they can allow him in," he looks at me. "Everything is filled to capacity."

He grabs the phone with one hand, without letting go of mine, and I see that he hits redial.

I slowly reach for the phone, hang up, and set the phone on the coffee table.

"I know you like to fix things for everyone," I say gently. "But this isn't one of those things, Levi."

"I don't know how to just sit here and do nothing," he says, choking up, now staring at his phone.

"I know," I tell him.

"And on top of it all, I have this stupid thing tonight." He leans his head back against the couch.

Nervous, I say, "We've been around Marcia. We should be quarantining ourselves."

"You'd think," he says with a look of disgust in his eyes. "Sullivan had the winners sign a waiver and a NDA."

I shake my head. "Wow," that is all I can say.

"Yep." He pauses. "I'm sorry about last night by the way," he says.

I look down, avoiding his gaze, hating once again that he was arguing with Max because of me. "Can I ask you something?"

"Sure," he says as he starts to rub small circles on my hand.

I pause. My breath catching. "Max said you didn't care about what tabloids and all said before, but you do now. Why?"

He sighs. "Because before, it was just me they were going after, and I can tune that stuff out. What they said then wasn't hurting someone I care about.

21

LEVI

It's always been about the music. Not the fame, or the money, or everything that comes with it. The fans... I love them. I couldn't be more grateful because if it wasn't for them, I wouldn't be doing what I do today. So I love getting to meet them, signing stuff, taking pictures... If I can make their day by doing that, I'm happy. Now, Sullivan... all he cares about is what the band can do for him. He doesn't care about the fans, he most definitely doesn't care about any of us, and this auction thing tonight – it's plain bullshit. Tonight is different from the usual meet and greets. For the first time, tonight will be like playing a part, so I put on the ripped jeans and black t-shirt. Okay, nothing new there, but then I grab my leather jacket and sunglasses and it's like hiding behind a guy the media created.

"Ready?" Kev asks from the door. "I have a mask for

you," he says as he raises his hand. "I don't trust Sullivan's test." He throws the black mask my way.

"Thanks, man," I say, catching the mask mid-air.

"What's wrong with you?" He asks.

"Shitty day," I tell him and he chuckles. "What!" He gasps. "Levi O'Connor doesn't have bad days. Like ever."

I sigh, "Marcia caught the virus and is in the hospital. And Riley might leave soon."

Even saying it out loud hurts. I felt like she was keeping something after I told her about Marcia, but I finally got her to say what was on her mind.

"Shit," he says. "Because of last night?"

"Nah. It's about the lockdown being extended. There is no word on what they'll do about her audition now. She wants me to talk to mom to see if this is the right move or if she should stay."

"What are you going to do?" He asks.

"I want to lie and say it is a horrible fucking idea and that she needs to stay."

Kev smiles. "I wouldn't call that a lie. Tell her it is a horrible fucking idea and that she needs to stay because you want her here."

I sigh and run my fingers through my hair. "I don't know how you and Ginny managed to keep your relationship a secret for this long. It's been what? Like a year already?"

"Getting there," he says. "It's not easy. We kinda made a game out of sneaking around. But then again, the paparazzi don't love me as much as they love you."

"Wanna trade?" I joke.

"Nope."

I hear a familiar rough voice coming from the hallway before I see Xavier stand behind Kev. He's wearing a suit, sunglasses, and is holding a juice box, which is always funny for some reason. I mean, the guy is the typical giant security guard, and he can probably finish that juice in one sip.

"Who had the bright idea of letting the stalker from last year know where you live? Wait. Don't tell me. Lucifer."

"The one and only," Kev says.

"Well, I briefed the front desk. Once she leaves, she isn't allowed back. I swear, I need a raise," he says.

"You do," Kev and I say at the same time. "I'll make sure you get one," Kev continues.

"Well, let's get this over with," I say.

RILEY

"Why, Wilson?? Whyyyy?" I ask as he begs to go outside. I can't take him to the rooftop because of the auction thing. I can't take him to the front because of the damn paparazzi.

"Here," says Krissy as she rummages through her clothes. She turns around with two hoodies and sunglasses in hands. She gives me one of each, then grabs a mask out of the top of the dresser and throws it my way.

"What's this?" I ask her.

"We're taking him out back and hoping no-one is

there. Lucky us, the masks cover half our faces. Just put it on."

She notices I am far from okay with this plan.

"You can stay with Wilson by the staff elevator while I check out the area to make sure it is clear."

I let out the breath I was holding and look at Wilson's impatient expression.

"Okay," I finally agree.

I stay by the employee elevator with Wilson as Krissy goes to look around. I offer to go with her, but she refuses, saying she hasn't been all over the tabloids like I have, so she'll be fine.

I hate garages.

They are dark, creepy, and now, every little noise I hear, from car doors to just about everything, makes me jump. After a while, I look at the time on my phone. Five minutes have gone by. I text her.

Me: Everything okay? I'm coming after you.

Krissy: Stay. I'll be back soon. I'm ok.

More time passes, and I start to get worried, and Wilson lays down on the ground, bored.

Me: I'm on my way out.

I'm about to hit send when she comes running in my direction.

She looks different. She has this spark in her eyes like she just saw something she shouldn't have. "Area is clear now," she says out of breath, "but you need to see this first." She practically shoves the phone in my face.

"Do you know who that is?" She asks and I nod. "Their manager." I continue to watch intently as he hands the blonde girl in the whorish mini - mini dress a bag of pills. "Just put it in their drinks. You'll have the time of your life. Far more than what you – well, than what I paid for so you could win the auction."

"I can't believe this," I say.

"Right? I was filming because if I had a run in with some crazy person or paparazzi, I wanted to be damn sure I was going to have it on video, and then –"

I cut her off, already hitting the button for the elevator. "We need to tell them," I say.

I get in the elevator, lower the hood and remove my sunglasses, leaving the mask on. Krissy does the same, and then I press the button to the rooftop.

"So, here is the plan," she says. "If there is security, we tell them we need to take Wilson to the garden. We keep an eye on things until we get an opportunity to tell one of the guys."

I start fidgeting with Wilson's leash. "Okay," I tell her. "And if they don't let us in?" I ask.

"They sure as hell better let us."

That is the longest elevator ride of my life. I'm worried for Levi and the guys. But mostly, I'm scared of what I will find. Wilson knows my anxiety is building up. He leans against my leg and I start petting his head, slowly calming my heartbeats as I do.

The moment the elevator door opens, a guy in a suit

turns to face us, and Wilson immediately starts growling. "Hell. We're not going to get through him," I mumble under my breath when the manager, who is next to the security guy, also faces us.

"What are you doing here?" The security guy asks, blocking my view. Krissy reaches for my hand and grabs Wilson's leash. "The dog has to go out. Thanks to you," she says. "We can't take him out front."

"Why not?" He asks and Krissy points at me. "Meet Sleeping Beauty,"

"Oh." The guy says as he gives me a friendly smile and pets Wilson. I notice then, it wasn't him that Wilson was growling at, but their manager. *'That makes sense.'*

"Yeah. Oh," Krissy mocks him as she rolls her eyes. He grins, looking amused. "We just need to get him to the garden and then we'll be out of here."

The guy looks at the manager, who looks to his right, past the bar, and says to let us pass. The moment the security guy moves, I can see Levi and the guys getting their pictures taken with four women. I notice Kev holding on to his mask and he keeps glancing at it. He is far from fine by having it off. The blonde one with Levi is all over him.

All. Over. Him.

Arms wrapped around his waist, practically humping his leg, and he looks – he looks like he has never been more uncomfortable.

Levi looks directly at me then and keeps his gaze locked on mine as the blonde girl keeps nuzzling into his shoulder and moves her left hand on his chest. I feel like I stop breathing for a moment when he reaches for her hand, but he only does that to move her hand away from him. Still, the pit in my stomach grows as Krissy, Wilson and I walk toward the back so we can get to the garden. Never once, do I take my eyes off him or him off me.

"That, my friend," says Krissy, "is the look he gave you after that kiss in the video… the one you refuse to watch."

"I – I –"

"Exactly," says Krissy.

We get to the garden's entrance and Wilson immediately raises his leg near the bush. "Wish he had peed on their manager," I mumble and Krissy laughs.

"Shit. That girl is getting mad," Krissy says, and I notice the blonde's furious expression as Levi ignores her, still locking his gaze with me. That is when I notice that she lets go of his waist and reaches for his hand and starts to pull him toward the bar, where there is a row of shots lined up.

"Now what?" I ask Krissy.

"Now Wilson and I distract the manager and security and you talk to Levi, since he is the only one done with the photo ops. I sent you the video so we have backup. Just show it to him."

"Okay," I tell her, but I can't make myself move. Feeling like I can't breathe, I take the mask off.

"Riley, do I need to use that damn third decision-making boss-pass on this?" Krissy says urgently, but she doesn't need to. As I notice the woman next to Levi reach in her purse, I'm already on the move. I see the manager coming toward me as Krissy intercepts. Levi is facing the bar. His back to me. I tap his shoulder. He turns and the moment his lips part, I lean in and kiss him. I start to pull away when I feel someone's grip on my wrist and shouts of lawsuit for breach of– when Levi pulls me back in: one hand on the side of my neck, another on the small of my back, pulling me toward him, and as he deepens the kiss my arms go around him.

He pulls away just enough to whisper, "Please don't leave," against my lips. He moves in for more when we hear, "Levi O'Connor, I swear to God. If you cause me and the label to lose more money."

I pull back then, and it takes me a minute to get my bearings on my surroundings. The security guy is holding the blonde woman back, and the other girls have cameras on. *'Jesus. Here we go again.'* Meanwhile, Krissy shows her phone to Bentley and Kev.

Levi laces his fingers through mine. "What's happening?" He asks as the guys walk toward us and show him the video while the blonde girl continues to make threats.

We all look at Sullivan.

"What?" Sullivan asks.

"You are so fucking fired," Max grins as the security guy asks Bentley to have the girls stop streaming.

Surprisingly, they do.

"What the hell for? All I do is keep you children out of trouble. And you can't even honor an auction contract that we will now be sued for," Sullivan growls.

"It's not a valid contract," Levi says and Sullivan glares at him. "The winners couldn't be associated with the band in any way. I do believe that being set-up by the manager, who paid for their wins, fucking fits the description. Not to mention that you gave someone roofies to put in our drinks. Roofies... really, Sullivan?" Levi growls. "Is that how you get laid?"

"Dad is going to disown your ass," Bentley says.

Sullivan's eyes widen as he looks at the security guy. "No one leaves without signing NDAs," he warns.

"Please ask the girls to sign it, Xavier," Levi asks him. "Then they can go. Make sure they get their pictures from tonight and the signed stuff the label sent, please."

Bentley pulls Sullivan to the side and starts yelling at him, with Max, Kev, Krissy, and even Wilson as backups. Levi wraps me in his arms and rests his chin on top of my head. "You're not leaving, right?" He asks.

I shake my head.

"Thank you," he says in a whisper.

"What for?" I ask, confused.

"For not leaving, and for helping us get rid of that fucker," he says as he pulls away. "I love music, but this circus – mostly because of his decisions, were making me start to hate what I do."

"I'm not signing shit," Krissy tells Xavier, grabbing our attention. Wilson barks in support of her decision.

Sullivan tilts his head to the side. "No one is leaving until that NDA is signed. I'm not ruining my career because of this."

"First," Krissy says as she puts a hand on her hips. "I got literally nowhere to go, so that doesn't bother me one bit. Second, I'm pretty sure you ruined your career all on your own."

"I think it's time for you to go," Levi tells Sullivan and after Xavier gets the auction winners in the elevator, he comes in Sullivan's direction, stands next to him, and says, "We can do this the easy way or the hard way, and I'm more than fine with either option."

"I own this fucking building," Sullivan says.

"Correction," Bentley snarls. "Dad owns the building, and he is next on my list of calls."

Sullivan just glares at him. "Fine," he snaps. "But if that video sees the light of day, you all will pay for it."

22

RILEY

"I CANNOT BELIEVE THIS IS HAPPENING!" Krissy says excitedly as we sit down by the bar on the rooftop. After Xavier contacted his friend at the police station to give him the video, he told us all to stay put while he checks out the building to make sure the girls – especially the stalker – and Sullivan left. Oh, and he took Wilson with him. Apparently, he thinks that Wilson would do a good job at finding hiding stalkers and evil managers.

"What?" I ask Krissy. My head is pounding after tonight's events. "Are you talking about your awesome skills at getting hidden footage and then using it for the greater good?"

She looks like she's deep in thought for a split second as she glances over toward Bentley, then she looks up at me. "No," she says. "I mean, yeah, that was awesome, but I'm talking about you kissing Levi. What does that mean? Are you guys –"

Levi cuts her off and puts an arm around me. For a split second, the pressure in my head lifts and then it starts pounding again. "Dating?" He asks. "I sure hope so."

"Your mom is going to kill me," I say truthfully as I rub small circles against my temples.

Levi reaches for my hands and lowers them. "Nah. She'll want to kill me though, but nothing new there." He grins without a care in the world, raises my hand to his lips and kisses it. "She'll be fine after a few days. In fact, the sooner I tell her the better. She can get over it while on the road and be fine before she gets here."

"Please don't," I tell him. "I'm not ready for that. Besides, it's quite possible you will get bored of me by the time she gets back," I joke.

He doesn't laugh.

"I'm serious about this, Riley, about us. Do you know when the last time I dated someone was?" He asks.

Krissy laughs. "Based on the tabloids… never. It seems like you've been living the male whore lifestyle for a while."

He glares at her.

"Not helping," he tries to look serious, but I can see the hint of a smile. "And I thought you were on my team."

Krissy reaches over the bar and grabs a coke. "I'm on Riley's team. Now, please. Go on. When was the last time you were serious about dating someone?"

"Never," he says.

I wait for the smile, or the laugh, or any indication that he's kidding. That doesn't come.

Now Krissy is the one glaring, also studying his expression.

"Looks like you got an inexperienced one, Riley," she laughs and I shake my head, thinking to myself – *definitely not less experienced than me.*

He shrugs. "I just never met someone before that I could see myself with for the long run."

I gape. Krissy gapes. *How can he just say stuff like that?*

Krissy opens the coke. "You're just a walking love song, aren't you? Krissy jokes, and I shift uncomfortably.

"Shit," he says. "I'm scaring you, aren't I?"

"It – it's just that we only met a few days ago," I stammer, but even saying that feels wrong. I feel the connection. As much as I tried to fight it, it's there. Before when I said I was leaving… I regretted it as soon as the words left my lips.

He grabs Krissy's soda and takes a sip, then hands it back to her.

She shakes her head. "Yeah… you can keep that."

He shrugs and looks at me. "It's fine. Different personalities. I realized how I felt from day one. You're still trying to fight how you feel about me. You'll get there." He gives me a crooked smile.

"Cocky much," says Krissy, rolling her eyes at him.

LEVI

"I guess things are back to normal in Levi's world," Bentley says as he walks toward us. I still have my arms wrapped around Riley, and I can't remember the last time I was this freaking happy. So much so that the happiness I feel right now wiped the brewing headache from earlier today.

"What do you mean?" Krissy asks.

Bentley looks at Krissy, now standing next to him. "You know those annoying people that have incredibly good luck most of the time? Things just magically work out for them?"

Krissy nods.

"That's Levi. Yeah, I know his day didn't start well and he's worried sick about Marcia, but getting rid of my brother and getting the girl on the same day – not bad." I can feel Riley tense under my hold, and I just pull her closer.

"Ha Ha." I say, thinking about how I need to call to see if there are any updates on Marcia.

The elevator door opens and I'm starting to really hate that sound. I relax when I see Xavier and Wilson come out, along with Joe – the guy who works at the front desk. They are both carrying the blankets I texted Xavier about.

"What's going on with that?" Max asks. When I turn to glare at him, I see Kev on the phone, probably calling Ginny. "And can I go now?" he says in an annoyed tone. "Last I checked only Levi is on house arrest."

"Funny," I say. "Any way. I don't know about you, but I need to recover from the past few days. We have the snacks from the meet and greet. We could play some music and camp up here."

I lean down toward Riley and my lips brush her ear as I murmur, "And cross two things off your list with camping and a private concert."

23

LEVI

When I finally look at my phone, I see that tonight's kiss is on social media, and so was the beginning of the interaction with Lucifer. The rumors are flying! What will happen to Oblivion now? Are they breaking up? And some shitty comments about Riley interrupting the meet and greet, which I'm now glad that she isn't on social media to read them.

Xavier went down to stay at the apartment for tonight and took Wilson with him. We have our area on the rooftop set. No drums tonight, but we have a plan. Ginny got a cab over, and now the girls are sitting on the blankets in the middle of the garden while we are sitting on a straight row of chairs. I am holding my guitar. The guys are ready to sing, and the best part is that Lucifer can't stop us from doing this. Sing just to sing. We're going to stream live as a small appreciation for the fans – simply because we want to.

Ginny grabs Kev's phone and starts streaming.

"Hey Lovelies," I say as I position my guitar. "I know there are a lot of rumors flying around tonight. I just wanted to say that we are not going anywhere." I plan to address the thing with Riley later, because I know she doesn't want to be the spotlight, especially sitting right here. "What happened tonight is actually a good thing, because now, there is no-one to stop us from doing this little concert for you."

I feel Kev's glare because yeah, he worries too much and there is the label who our contract is with but, hell. The four of us agreed we'd make this a charity thing and if they complain, that makes them look bad. So I ask the fans to make a donation of any amount they can to any organization helping with the virus in some way or another.

This feels good. It feels really freaking good. And so freeing. I can sense the shift in our energy. Tonight, we sing like we haven't in a long time, and seeing the look in Riley's eyes as she watches me sing, only makes it better.

Tonight feels like a new beginning.

When we are done and Ginny stops streaming, I stand up and walk toward Riley, extending my hand to help her up. Then I pull her into a hug.

"What did you think?" I ask her.

"Not bad," she pauses. "Bentley and Kev are pretty good," she says playfully.

"Hey!" Max and I say at the same time as I pull away.

"You guys are amazing," she says. "That was fun. Thank you."

"You don't have to thank me," I tell her. "I'll sing to you any time."

"And that," Max interrupts, "is my cue to leave. Besides, I have to feed the dogs."

We say bye to Max and the others stay. They sit around on the blankets and I pull Riley toward one of the daybeds and I sit down, pulling her down so she is sitting between my legs.

Bentley grabs the guitar and starts singing and we all just sit back and listen.

Riley is leaning against me, and after a while, I feel her shift.

Krissy, sitting next to Bentley, smiles at me and puts a finger against her mouth to shush me and then motions to tell me Riley is sleeping.

She fell asleep in my arms. I smile. And this right here is everything. I'm almost afraid to move because I don't want to wake her up.

After a while, Krissy goes back to the apartment, the guys leave, and I stay right where I am.

When her phone rings at about three in the morning, I quickly fumble with it in an attempt to quiet it so not to wake her up, but I hit the wrong button and answer it.

"Hmm, Hi," I say as I position the phone, and the person on the screen can see me, the garden behind us, and just the top of Riley's head.

'Fuck. I hope this isn't her mom. That would be a hell of a first impression.'

The woman on the line looks tired. She has a scarf on her head, and I remember Riley telling me about her aunt.

"Ah. The rockstar," she says.

I smile. I can't help it.

"She talks about me?" I ask quietly to not wake her up.

"Maybe," she jokes. "I'm Lilly by the way."

"Great meeting you, Lilly. I'm Levi. So, I hear you're Riley's favorite person," I say.

That puts a HUGE smile on her face.

"The one and only. Well, scratch that. Maybe not the only one. You may have a fair chance at that favorite spot."

"Wouldn't dream of it," I tell her. "I'll be happy with second favorite."

She smiles again. "You taking care of my favorite niece? Making sure she has fun, but not too much fun?" She raises an eyebrow at me.

"Trying my best," I grin. "Just the right amount of appropriate fun, of course." I say as I grin.

She nods and smiles.

"What?" I ask. "I'm being honest. Full transparency here."

"I believe you," she tells me. "Just thinking about how people come into our lives at just the right time is all."

I nod because she's right.

"You take care of my favorite niece, rockstar," she says.

"Do you want to talk to her? I can wake her up," I put my hand against her arm and start to shift under her.

"Nah. It's okay," her aunt says, but I can tell by her voice that is far from okay.

"I think she'll be mad if I don't," I say.

And she laughs. "You're probably right."

"Riley, your aunt is on the phone." She smiles sleepily. I hold the phone up to her and she says "Hey, Aunt Lilly."

Riley is nowhere near awake and can barely keep her eyes open.

"Hey, favorite niece. Go ahead and get some rest, okay? I just wanted to say hi and tell you that I love you," She pauses, and I glance down to see if she hung up, but she's still there, watching Riley sleep. "And by the way," she continues. "The rockstar has my approval."

"The rockstar is trouble," Riley says sleepily, and I chuckle. "Love you too, favorite aunt."

24

(DAY 5)

RILEY

WHEN I OPEN MY EYES, the sun is rising, and all I can hear is his heartbeat. I can feel his arm around me and the last thing I want to do is move.

It takes me a few seconds to realize where I am. I take in the plants around us, the other daybeds, and I slowly start to sit up. I roll my neck back and forth - my whole entire body aching and my head still pounding. I look at Levi and I cannot believe I fell asleep on him.

I see the grin forming on his lips before he opens his eyes. "Good morning, Sleeping Beauty," he says sleepily as he yawns and stretches his arms.

"I'm sorry –" I start to apologize.

"For what?" He asks, leaning toward me. He steals a kiss and my breath catches.

"For falling asleep like that," I whisper against his lips. "You could have woken me up."

I feel his hand on the small of my back.

"No way in hell," he says a little more awake now. "I wouldn't have changed a thing about last night."

I blush. At least I think I do and the grin on his face confirms it. I don't think I will ever get used to him blurting out stuff like this.

"Can I ask you something?" He says.

"You mean something else?" I joke.

He chuckles, "Yeah. I'm just wondering why you made that comment yesterday about thinking that I will get bored."

I look down, avoiding his gaze. "I'm likely the opposite of every girl you've ever been with. You're used to girls throwing themselves at you. You're spontaneous and you just go for things and I… don't," I pause watching the way he's looking at me, hanging on to my every word. "I like you," I tell him, and I notice his dimples form as he grins. "A lot. But as hot as you are, I am not jumping in bed with you like that."

He gives me a crooked smile. "You do think I am hot."

"Ugh," I groaned. "That's all you heard?"

"Nah," he chuckles. "Did you ever stop to wonder if maybe that is one of the things I love about you?"

"What? The chase?" I laugh.

I expect him to laugh or make a joke out of it, but he looks serious as he stares at me with an intensity that sends shivers through my body. "The possibility of having something real… of having more. I honestly can't tell you the last time I had a real conversation with someone – you know – like we do." He pauses. "I'm not in a rush, Riley. I'm all in, and I am good with taking things slow. You set the pace. I follow your lead."

I tilt my head to the side. "So if I told you I wanted to wait until marriage to –"

He cuts me off, "I'd say when are we getting married?" Of course, by the expression on his face, he is joking, and I laugh at his response.

He leans forward, brushes a lock of my hair behind my ear, then moves in closer, brushing his lips against mine, and whispers, "Stop trying to push me away, Riley."

When we walk into the apartment, there is a message on the door that I have a package that needs to be picked up and signed for at the front desk. We find Xavier sleeping on the couch with Wilson, who wags his tail then goes back to sleep. Levi takes a few pictures of them and kisses my forehead before he plops down on the other couch while I grab a mask and go pick up the package.

By the front door, there are two people looking in, holding cameras.

I turn my back to them.

"I guess they think the lockdown doesn't apply to them," the woman at the front desk says in an annoyed tone as she hands me an envelope. I sign for it, and when I turn to go back to the elevator, I see one of the guys outside position his camera, and I quickly turn and rush to the elevator.

I open the envelope then.

Inside, there is a printout of a tabloid with tomorrow's date on it, and on the front page, there is a quote from an open letter written by Levi – about me. In huge bold letters, it reads, "She comes first."

Infuriated, I march into the living room. He is still sitting on the couch, now snuggling with MY dog. *Little traitor. He's lucky he is cute. My dog, not* – ugh. *Focus, Riley!*

He looks at me. "Yes?" He asks.

"I don't get why you're doing this," I say, thrusting the paper into his hand. "I'm never going to get out of the spotlight now, am I? And when did you even have time to do this? Do these people not sleep?" I want to stay mad, but there is that hint of a smile on his lips. Ugh. I sigh. "Look. There are no cameras. No one is following you around. Likely for once in your life, there is no one around that you have to impress."

He grabs the paper and tosses it down on the coffee table. "Maybe I'm trying to impress you." He stands as he gives me a devilish grin.

"You already have me," I say as I cross my arms over my chest.

He just stares at me, until I finally relax. The moment when I uncross my arms, he reaches for my hand and pulls me toward him. His arms instantly wrap around my waist. "Fine!" I say, tilting my head back. "Okay. That was sweet of you to defend my role in the rooftop fiasco and all. But unnecessary."

His grin widens as he leans in for a kiss. "I will never stop trying to impress you, Riley Andrews. Be ready for a lifetime of crazy."

LEVI

Did I have to write that open letter? No. But I'd be damned if I let those comments about Riley interrupting the meet and greet fly without defending her. Besides, she was sleeping curled into me and I was inspired to write it.

It's important to me that my fans know that she's here to stay, and that last night's events weren't what they seemed. Mostly, it is important they know that she inspires me. She inspires me to write. She inspires me to play. She inspires me to do what I love doing in a whole new way. The musician in me chuckles at the lame rhyme.

After Riley goes back to the rooftop to dance, I sit back down on the couch next to Wilson and return the many missed calls from mom.

"Levi Jameson," she yells into my ear, making Wilson get up and walk away. I wish I could do the same… "Break it off. Before I get home tomorrow morning."

"Tomorrow?" I asked, confused.

"Yes, tomorrow. Since you obviously need a babysitter."

"Riley could –"

She cuts me off. "Do not even finish that sentence, Levi Jameson."

"Can't break it off," I tell her. "It's too late."

"What the hell do you mean, too late, Levi? She is staying at my house. She is my responsibility!"

"I like her," I say, thinking, *'No, it's more than that, but my mom doesn't get to know that kind of thing about my life.'*

And she laughs, before she goes into a rage about me being irresponsible and reckless, and her being ashamed of my lifestyle and how everything about it will hurt Riley and everything she has worked for.

I've had to learn to not let these things get to me, but it is draining.

"I fully support what she came here to do and her career path, even though it's the same path you took," I say that last part in a sarcastic tone. "But I'm not going to stop seeing her, mom," I say. "If you have to lock me in my room until I'm off of house arrest so she can stay and do what she came here for, so be it. But I'm not letting her go."

The line goes silent.

"We'll talk about this later." And she hangs up on me. I look up to see Xavier smiling across from me.

"At least some things never change," Xavier says, referring to my mom's famous lectures.

"Yeah," I say. "Tomorrow is going to be hell."

"Good for you, though," he says. "Riley seems like a nice girl for a change. Less work for me." He laughs and I throw a pillow at him.

Next to me, another phone rings and I realize it's Riley's.

I answer it without even looking to see who is calling. Thinking of Riley's aunt makes me smile. There is just an aura about her. She is one of those people who can make others happy just by talking to them for a while, and I look forward to talking to someone nice after the disastrous call with mom.

"Hi Aunt Lilly," I say with a smile.

Only, it is not her aunt.

"Who are you?" the woman asks. My eyes widen and I

shift nervously. I can tell she is Riley's mom. She has the same blonde hair, the same brown eyes, and facial features.

"Mrs. Andrews?" I ask and she nods.

"I'm Levi," I give her a nervous smile and just blurt out the first thing that comes to mind, because that is what I do during the rare instances when I'm nervous. "And I like your daughter."

25

LEVI

I STAND by the elevator for who knows how long, watching Riley dance where the bar tables and chairs were. She looks so peaceful – happy. And she's listening to my song. The one I composed years ago. The one song I was proud of at the time. That was before I got the guts to stand up for myself and leave to do what I wanted to do.

I thought mom coming home would be hell. I was wrong. This is. The call with Riley's mom went from "I like your daughter" to a cold "I need to talk to Krissy." And I get it. After Krissy told me what happened, I knew the least I could do was offer to tell Riley. Krissy was in no condition of being able to do that. So here I am. Standing here. And I don't want to be the one to take that happiness away from her. I don't even want to be standing here watching that happiness vanish.

The song ends, and Riley's expression suddenly shifts completely. The smile is already gone before she sees me standing, leaning against the wall by the elevator.

And then, she sees me. And the smile doesn't reappear.

I put my hands in my pockets and walk over toward her. I keep my head down because I can't even bear to look into her eyes right now. It's as if she will read right through me if I do.

I pull my hand out of my pocket when I reach her and slip my hand into hers.

"Come with me," I say. Even the sound of my own voice doesn't sound right. She notices it too because she doesn't ask questions. She just follows me quietly as I lead her toward the bench by the garden's entrance.

We both sit down. And I can't for the life of me find the words.

"What's wrong?" She finally asks. "Is Marcia okay?"

"Yeah," I say. My voice breaking. "I called earlier. Her husband said she's showing small signs of improvement." I pause. "Riley," I say, looking at our hands.

I pause again.

I let out a breath I was holding. "Your mom called," I say as I look at her, and the tears are already welling up in her eyes. That is the moment I know that she knows, but there is still hope in there too as she waits for me to go on. I can see in her eyes she needs confirmation, but at the same time, is hoping that isn't it. "Your Aunt Lilly," I start to say as she closes her eyes, tilts her head down and I pull her toward me, putting my arms around her as she cries.

And I stay here. For as long as she needs me.

RILEY

My mind is just a complete fog. I knew this was coming. In a weird way, I felt her presence when I was dancing this morning. Still, it doesn't feel real. I knew it would hurt when it happened, but this pain is incomparable to what I attempted to prepare myself for.

"Krissy," I say in between sobs.

"I can go get her," Levi says, not letting go.

I shake my head. "Please stay," I say against his chest, gripping on to his shirt.

"What can I do?" Levi asks softly.

"Just be here," I tell him. "I wish I could be with my mom right now. I hate that she's alone."

Levi pulls away then and reaches for his phone.

"Do you have a passport?" He asks and I nod.

He goes back to typing and texting.

"What are you doing?" I ask. My voice barely audible.

"I'm getting you to your mom," he says. "And I'm asking the band's doc to come and do one of those rapid tests so you are clear."

"Thank you," I say. And I just wish he could come with me.

Things move fast. I'm packed by the time the doctor gets here and the plane is set to leave in three hours.

I don't miss the pissed off look in the doctor's face when Levi opens the door. The doctor looks like he just got out of med school and would rather be anywhere but here. Literally. He is wearing shorts, flip flops, a Hawaiian shirt and looks like he's ready for vacation. "Mask up if you want me to come in," he says.

Levi grabs a mask that was by the front door and looks back at me to make sure I have one too. I was already holding one, so I just put it on. The doctor's mood doesn't improve any when he finds out the test is for me. Levi had told him the test was for himself, just to get him here fast. We are five minutes into waiting on the results when the doctor, who is sitting on the couch across from us, rubs his hand against his forehead. "You need one too," he tells Levi.

"No, I don't," he says. "I wish I was going with her but," he points toward his ankle monitor.

"No, you need one." The doctor says in a firm tone.

"Is it an insurance thing?" Levi asks, confused. "To hide that this is actually for her?"

"Fuck it," the doctor says. "I swear this job is the source of all my ethical dilemmas."

Levi lets go of my hand and leans forward.

"What is this about?" He asks in a stern tone.

The doctor puts both hands up. "In my defense, I was told a winner would be disqualified if their test was positive, until I saw on social media that was not the case."

"What are you talking about?" Levi growls.

"One of the winners from the auction tested positive."

I freeze. I thought I was too numb to feel anything. I was wrong. And now, it all makes sense. The headache, the body ache… I know the results before they are confirmed.

“It’s positive,” the doctor says. Then he looks at Levi. “And so is yours.”

26

LEVI

WELL. Shit.

I didn't think Riley could look any more heartbroken, but she does. And it shatters me.

"Do you mind if I use Carly's room to call my mom?" She asks without meeting my eyes. "I probably shouldn't be around Krissy."

"Yeah. Of course." I assure her. I look over at the doc, who is practically bathing in hand sanitizer. "Do you have more tests? I think it is safe to say that the guys and Krissy need it too."

"Yeah," he says, adjusting the side of his mask. "I can give Krissy's and then swing by their house on my way home."

"Thank you," I say as I run my fingers through my hair thinking of the number of people that could have it because of that dumbass. "And Xavier too. I think he's out walking the dog."

"Sure thing," the doc says before I yell out for Krissy.

I sit here – at a safe distance, as Krissy and Xavier – both now wearing masks, wait for their test results. Time drags, and all I can do is stare toward the bedroom door.

"Negative," doc tells them. "For now anyway."

"My parents are going to freak," Krissy says. "What now? I don't want to go back home."

"Well. You can quarantine in separate rooms," the doctor suggests. "Or if the guys come back negative, you could probably stay at their house for a while."

Krissy nods, but for the first time since I met her, she looks sad and scared, and to make it even worse, she is quiet.

"Do you mind staying here for a bit?" I ask the doc. "I may need you to verify this."

He gives me a confused look but stays where he is while I call mom.

I put her on speaker.

"Hey mom."

"Hey kid," dad says. I can tell by the background that I'm on speaker too. That is what she does when she's mad at me. Which is quite often.

"You behaving these past few hours?" He asks and I can picture mom glaring at him.

"Trying to," I say. "I have some bad news."

"Oh?" He says at the same time mom growls, "What now?"

I sigh. "There is no easy way to say this, but you can't come home. Riley and I tested positive for the virus."

There is silence. Long. Uncomfortable. Silence.

"You there?" I finally say.

"You're making this up," she accuses.

I shake my head, even though she can't see me. "Why would I lie about that, mother?"

"To spend more time with Riley would be my first guess."

I look over at the doc and motion toward the phone.

"The doc is here," I tell her. "He can confirm it." I hand him the phone and go to the room.

The bedroom door is open when I get there. Riley is sitting on the bed talking to her mom. She's leaning her back against the headboard and has her legs stretched out. I don't think she even realizes it, but she points her toes up and down as she talks to her mom, as if subconsciously doing a ballet exercise. When she notices me watching from the door, she nods for me to come in. I do, but stay quiet and out of the camera view. I lay down next to where she's sitting and put my arm over her lap, scooting as close as possible to her, and I close my eyes.

I listen to them talking about how her aunt wanted to be cremated and have her ashes spread at some park in Thailand.

When I feel her fingers combing through my hair, I let out a long breath.

Given the last few conversations I've had today I expected Riley – more than anyone else – to be pissed as fuck about it all. She has every reason to be. This is really going to impact her training and her ability to see her mom.

"Be safe sweetheart," her mom says, and I assume she didn't tell her she was positive.

"Okay," she says. "I love you."

"I love you too."

Riley hangs up the phone but doesn't stop playing with my hair.

"You didn't tell her," I say.

"She has enough going on already. I told her I'd have to quarantine to travel so it doesn't make sense for me to go. By the time I got to be with her, she would be back."

I move, laying my head on her lap and looking up at her.

"I'm sorry, Riley. If it wasn't for me –"

"We're not doing that." She interrupts. "This wasn't your fault."

"But –"

"But nothing." Her face is getting red and I can tell by her tone that she's getting more and more frustrated. "You can't control what your manager did. He's a shitty person and that was that."

She closes her eyes for a moment and takes a deep breath. "How's Krissy?" She asks, changing the subject.

"Her test was negative," I say.

"Thank God," she says, relieved.

"The doctor suggested we quarantine in a separate room to keep Krissy safe. She doesn't want to leave. You can stay here," I tell her. "I can sleep on the floor," I pause, "or if you really want me to, I can stay in my parents' room."

"Okay," she agrees, and I look at her, waiting for her to go on. She doesn't.

"Ooookay to which one?" I ask.

She chuckles. "You can stay here. I think I can control myself," she rolls her eyes at me. "You don't have to sleep on the floor."

27

LEVI

BEING in bed with Riley like this is both heaven and hell. We spent the past few hours just watching movies. She cried in between, and no matter how many times she assured me this isn't my fault, I still feel guilty as hell. But I don't pull away because of it. In fact, I don't want to move, but about halfway through *Queen of the Damned* – one of the movies with the best, most kickass soundtracks I've ever heard – my stomach starts to growl.

Riley is leaning her head on my shoulder, so she hears it loud and clear. She laughs, and it makes the guilt a little more bearable.

"I guess I should go get us something to eat," I say and she shifts, so I can get up. "And take Wilson out."

"I texted Krissy. She's got Wilson."

"Food?" I ask.

"Nah. I'll grab something later. I'm just going to

change out of these clothes and put on something more comfortable." She tells me.

"Need help?" I grin and she shakes her head. "Don't push your luck," she says with a smile.

Not that it takes long to eat a pastrami sandwich, but still, I don't think I've ever eaten so fast in my life. I grab my phone from the coffee table long enough to see the message from Bentley that they are all good, and negative, before I shut my phone off and throw it on the couch.

When I go back to the room, I'm a little on autopilot. I take my shirt off, throw it on the desk, grab my guitar and sit on the bed.

I don't miss the double-take Riley does as she glances over her phone at me.

"Everything good?" I ask, noticing she has on these super soft pajama pants that rides low on her waist and a short black tank top, and fuck. Sleeping here was probably not my brightest idea.

"Yeah. Do you always play half naked?" She jokes.

I give her a crooked smile. "Depending on the audience."

She shakes her head, then sits up straighter against the headboard and starts to play with the tag on the blanket.

"They are going to announce an update about the scholarship and auditions sometime tomorrow. I just hope it's not before this quarantine is over."

"It won't be," I tell her. "They extended the lockdown again, so there's no way."

She looks from the tag to me. "What would you be

doing with your life if you weren't a famous rockstar?" She asks.

"Same as I do now. Just without the famous part," I laugh. "I don't know. I've never stopped to think about it. Maybe because I can't see myself doing anything else."

"What about you? I ask. "If you couldn't dance?" That is obviously something that is on her mind.

"I don't know," she says. "Right now, I feel like I'm racing against time. I have maybe what? 12 years or so as a dancer… and I feel like this virus is stealing time away from me."

I watch the long lost look in her eyes.

"And then after… I don't know. I could never teach. I would lose my mind," she laughs. "The thing I like about dance is the solitude even when other dancers are around. I can be dancing with a partner and still be in my own head. It's all muscle memory. My body moves without me thinking things through. It just happens. Teaching requires way too much interaction."

I adjust my hold on the guitar. "You could be a choreographer. Not teach, but just… you know? Create."

"Yeah. Maybe." She says but I can tell that for her, it is not the same.

"I get it," I tell her. "It would be like if I had to settle for teaching music instead of taking the stage to perform."

"Exactly." She sighs. "How are you feeling?"

I shrug. "Same as always. Maybe better because you are here," I smirk and she rolls her eyes at me. "Seriously though, I'm good. You?" I ask, putting the guitar back down and reaching for her hand.

"Same as always," she smiles. "Just a little headache. I feel like I'm going to lose my mind just staying in here though. I have to get to the rooftop and dance tomorrow. I just need to get my mind clear right now. But mostly, I'm scared. Which the whole mind clearing can help with."

"We are gonna be okay. Besides, I can help you clear your mind," I give her a crooked smile.

"How so?" She asks, grinning, "Another private concert?"

"Better." I say as I move enough to lean over her. I move my hand to the side of her waist, her tank top riding up – her skin feels warm under my hand. She thinks I'm about to kiss her. Instead, I quickly swoop my arm around her waist and move her so she's laying down. She gasps but doesn't pull away. I lean down and my lips brush against hers.

"Something like this," I murmur.

"I'm not sure this is distracting enough," she says out of breath, and I raise an eyebrow at her.

"Really?" I grin as I move in again, kissing her as I feel her arms go around my back – her fingers digging softly into my skin.

I don't know why this feels different, but I move slowly. With every move, I look for clues that she may want me to stop, or signs that I'm going too far. When I move my hand inside of her shirt and start to slowly move it up her back, I stop and look at her.

"You're hot," I say.

She shies away.

"Well, I mean – besides that you're hot in a sexy as hell way. You're burning up."

"I feel fine," she says.

"I know but," I pull away wondering when the hell did I start to become the responsible guy. "I'm going to go find a thermometer," I say.

'And then grab a cold shower,' I think to myself.

28

(DAY 6)

LEVI

'HOW TO BREAK A FEVER.' I type on Riley's phone, because I have no fucking clue.

Stay in bed and rest... done... *stay hydrated...* done... *fever reducing meds...* done. None of it has worked. *Stay cool by removing extra layers of clothing...* that stirs feelings in me that should not be stirring right now. *'What the fuck is wrong with me?'* I think to myself before I move on to the next one.

Take a tepid bath... cold baths can be dangerous. I'm about to need a fucking cold bath if these suggestions keep moving in the naked and wet direction.

I even turned up the heat and added an extra heater to the room and Riley still has the blanket up to her neck, trying to stay warm.

"Riley," I say, sitting next to her – on the edge of the bed. I put my hand to her forehead. She still feels hot.

She rubs her eyes, and looks at me, smiles, then closes them again. "I don't want to die a virgin," she mumbles, and I chuckle.

I reach for the water bottle next to the bed, watching her as she's completely out again. "Come on, Sleeping Beauty. Get up for a bit. You should drink some water."

She doesn't. I take her temperature again, and all humor leaves me.

"Okay, we need to get rid of this blanket," I say as I start to pull it down and remove it from the bed.

"But I'm cold!" She says, shivering, and when I lay down next to her, she instantly moves closer to keep warm. This is probably not helping with the whole break the fever thing, but I put my arms around her and bring her closer.

It's an inhuman hour when someone knocks on the door.

"Yes?" I ask.

"It's Krissy. Can you come out?"

I kiss Riley's forehead. Feeling relieved when she doesn't feel as warm. I slowly lift Riley's arm from around me, and get up, pulling a shirt over my head, grabbing a mask from the dresser and putting it on as I walk toward the door.

When I open it, Krissy is at a safe distance away.

She crosses her arms over her chest. *Okay...* "How is Riley?" She asks.

"I think the fever broke," I say in a low tone not to wake her. "What's up? And what time is it?"

"You need to see something." She says in a cold tone, ignoring my other question.

I nod and follow her to the living room keeping distance between us. She stops away from the coffee table and points at it.

There are three different tabloids on the table, and Riley and I are on the covers of each one of them. Three tabloids. Three different headlines. *'Jealous girlfriend goes after rockstar's fans.'* The first has a picture of the girl who won the auction with me and Riley walking our way, then a picture of Riley crying on the rooftop when she found out about her aunt, only, they made it look like she was crying because of me and the girl from the auction. The next one, *'Oblivion or Sleeping Beauty, which one will he choose?'* with a picture of us making out on the daybed, with some heavy photoshopping suggesting that we were doing way more. And the last, *'Ballerina gives up career for rockstar. Will he give up music for her?'* with a picture of Riley dancing on the rooftop, right next to a picture of me playing during the rooftop concert we streamed.

I rub my hand against my forehead and close my eyes, trying to think.

"This is fucked up," Krissy finally says, arms crossed.

"I don't understand how they even got these pictures."

"Does it matter?" Krissy snaps.

I stare at the magazines, shaking my head. "I guess not."

"Look, I get it that you like her. I get it that this isn't your fault. But this is going to hurt Riley. Especially that one," she points at the one with her dancing. "The school canceled auditions. They are going to base this year's selection on our portfolios and virtual brand. Do you know what they will find when they look up Riley? Nothing but this. They are going to think she is unfocused; that she is distracted by you and has too much baggage, and it is going to hurt her chances." Krissy pauses and her eyes go wide. "Shit" she says in a lower tone.

"Hey, Riley. How are you feeling?"

I quickly turn around. Riley has one of my t-shirts on, and her hair up in a messy bun. She looks better. But she isn't even looking at me. She's looking at the magazines. Tears surface in her eyes as she walks toward them. Then she stops. Her eyes widen, and I realize her face is getting red. She's starting to have another panic attack.

"Riley. Look at me," I say as I rush toward her, putting my hands on each side of her face and pulling her focus to me.

"Riley. Deep breaths," I say and I hear the wheezing when she shakes her head. And then, she passes out. I quickly scoop her up, cradling her in my arms, and lower her down on the couch. "Riley. Riley!" Nothing. I pick her back up and go toward the door, turning the knob and kicking the door open.

"What are you doing?" Krissy says frantically, "I'm calling 911."

"Call. I'm getting her downstairs and to a cab if they aren't here by the time I get there. If hospitals are full, I'm not sure how much calling will help." I say, knowing that I will storm in there and will get her seen one way or another.

“Levi,” Krissy says, and I quickly glance at her. She nods toward the ankle bracelet.

I turn back, and leave.

29

LEVI

THE MOMENT the elevator doors close, I hear her mumble my name.

"Thank God!" I say, looking down at her and feeling like I can breathe again, but I don't let her go. "How do you feel?"

She just puts her arms around my neck and closes her eyes again. It's like she can't stay awake.

When the elevator door opens, I rush toward the back of the building. Lock down or not, with this morning's news, the paparazzi are likely out there. I practically run carrying her for one block down before I turn to the busier intersection to grab a cab, only the streets are empty. No cabs in sight either. "Fuck." I stop, trying to figure out what to do, when a cop car pulls up in front of us. I'm ready to go off on the cop now standing in front of me. I don't know what I expected him to do, but what he did was definitely not it.

He looks like he's about my dad's age, average height, lean. I could probably… maybe outrun him, but I don't. Where would I even go? Run a few blocks to the hospital? But he looks concerned when he notices the terrified look in my eyes.

"What happened?" He asks, taking a few steps back and adjusting his mask.

"She has the virus. I don't know what's wrong, but she passed out earlier and she can't stay awake. I need to get her to the hospital."

"Levi Jameson O'Connor, right? Did you call 911?"

I nod. "Her friend did."

I can tell he's contemplating what to do.

"Come on," he says, and I start to follow him toward the car when I see three paparazzi with cameras catch up to us. I halt. What.The.Hell.

He sighs. I can see something in his eyes. Maybe frustration. As the paparazzi get closer, the officer steps in between us and them. "There is a lockdown in place. I suggest you go home. Now." He shifts his weight to block Riley's face from view, and surprisingly, they actually do as he demands. The moment they turn to leave, the cop faces me. "Give her to me and go back to your building. You're not going to help the situation outside. Not to mention that you won't be allowed in the hospital anyway."

"But –"

"I got her, son. Go back. You have a good reason for being out here. I won't take you in, but you need to get back to where you're supposed to be. I'll call the station, but if your monitor sends out another signal, someone will be here to get you," He pauses for a moment. "I'll come back after I take her in."

I don't want to leave her. I look down at her, and I can tell by the sweat running down her face that she's feverish again. I sigh. "Let me help get her in the car," I say and he nods, opening the back door.

I lower her on the seat, put the seat belt around and buckle her in, kiss her forehead and step away. I close the door slowly, hating that I have to leave her.

It's the longest hour of my life before the cop comes back. Xavier ran her ID and insurance card to the hospital, and Krissy waits with me in the living room. Both of us wearing masks and staying away from one another. Wilson is laying on the floor by the bedroom door and looks like the most depressed dog in the world and I know just how much he understands.

Xavier comes back with the cop, and this time, when the cop steps inside, I get his name. Officer Meija. I also make sure he knows I tested positive too.

"How is she?" I ask.

"She was awake for a little while but was having trouble breathing," he says. "I know that they called her mom, but that was about all they would tell me before they got swamped with incoming patients again."

Krissy is already on speaker with Mrs. Andrews by the time he finishes that sentence, and she starts sniffling in what I assume is the moment she sees Riley's mom on the screen.

"Can you make sure we're alone," her mom asks. Krissy looks from the phone to me, but nods and then disappears into the room.

For some reason, officer Meija stays.

"Am I in trouble?" I ask.

"No, son. I would just like to know how she's doing, if that's okay."

"Yeah. Of course. Have a seat. And thank you," I say, "for getting her there and for not taking me to jail. But mostly for getting her there."

"How did you get in this situation anyway?" He asks, looking toward the ankle monitor. I tell him everything from the night at the concert, to the negotiations to get me out of Europe, and on house arrest. He then asks me how I got into music.

He listens carefully. He pulls out a notepad when I mention Lucifer's name for the second, maybe third time, but puts the notepad right back in his pocket as Krissy comes out into the living room. She is a mess.

"How is she?" I ask desperately.

She hesitates and I have a gut-wrenching feeling.

"She's on a ventilator," she sobs, sitting on the couch and covering her face. Wilson rushes to her side and nudges her repeatedly as he whines, until she finally puts her arms around him. I stand up right away.

"Son," the cop says. "Don't do anything crazy. You can't get in the hospital," he reminds me. But I feel the tightness in my chest. I have to see her. I have to help in some way. "Just staying put is where you should be. It's all you can do anyway."

I take a deep breath and nod.

"You have to pretend you don't know anything," Krissy says. "I'll give you updates, but her mom was not the first one called. Your mom was the emergency contact on Riley's phone while her mom is overseas. She's the one who called Riley's mom. She apologized for your," she uses her hand to mimic quote marks, "role in getting Riley sick, the tabloids, and asked her to not give you any updates." Krissy lowers her hands and gives me a sympathetic look. "It's not your fault, Levi," she says as the blood drains from my face. I look straight at the cop – feeling empty.

"Maybe jail is better after all."

"No, it is not," he says. "But I may be able to help you. Just give me a few minutes."

I give him a confused look, but nod.

It's a good 20 minutes before he comes back, holding his phone.

"The universe is on your side today, Levi," he says, and I chuckle. "I seriously doubt that with Riley being at the hospital."

I hear a sarcastic, "I'm moving back home when I get fired," Before he turns the phone screen to me, "This is my daughter, Tara."

She looks like she's barely out of high school. *'I'm not in the right space to do this today,'* I think to myself. *'Whatever this is.'*

"Hmmm okay," I say, giving Tara an awkward wave, and we both go silent. He turns the camera back to himself. "You're better than this, kid. That's why you came to me with the situation to begin with," he tells her.

"Yeah, but I didn't give you every single detail... considering your job." She says, and Krissy and I keep looking back and forth at one another.

"Do the right thing," he tells her. "You were raised better than that."

He turns the phone back around and she sighs. He motions for me to take the phone, and I do.

"I work for one of those magazines that featured you this morning," she blurts out. "I'm not saying which one in hopes of saving my job because I do have bills. Sorry, Dad."

I swallow the lump in my throat and fight the urge to hang up.

"I did try to stop the article when I found out how the information came to us, but the editor said hell no. That's when I went to my dad, because I don't want to be personally involved with legal troubles. He said to stay out of it. I did, but they got another writer."

I lower my head and run my fingers through my hair. "How did they get footage?" I ask.

She's frowning. "Your manager hid cameras around the rooftop, then gave us what he had."

"Son of a bitch," Krissy and I say at the same time.

"Yep," Tara says and I can tell right away she doesn't like him.

I look at Krissy and get an idea. Turning back to Tara on the screen I ask, "Any chance you can get me that whole footage?"

She goes quiet. "Way above my pay grade to get my hands on that," she says.

I clench my fist. I can't believe I'm about to do this… "I'll give you an exclusive interview in exchange for all footage."

She straightens and she can't hide the smile, but she hesitates as if trying to figure out if I'm playing her.

"No questions off the table?" She asks.

"Nope."

"I'll see what I can do," she says with a smile.

I give her my private number, and then her dad cuts in. "What exactly did you leave out when you talked to me?" He demands.

"Ugh. Father." She sighs – the phone still in my hand and pointing at me. I hand it to him, but he says to put it on the coffee table, practically bathes the phone in Lysol, then picks it up so they can continue the conversation.

He gives her a look that says she better start speaking and fast.

"His manager likes to brag about things he shouldn't brag about. I think he was hoping this would end up in the papers at some point, and it probably would if the Riley story hadn't taken over. Then it became beneficial that it didn't."

"Explain." He demands.

"The whole house arrest thing started as a setup. Sullivan paid the guy to change a few details about the story, partially for publicity. He also had a deal with Levi's mom. Make things blow up, get him on house arrest and away from the band while Sullivan talked the label into replacing him with a new guy he signed. I guess the mom did a pretty good job at convincing the lawyer that house arrest would be the best solution. It's my understanding that she was involved in past publicity stunts to get the label to drop him. It just never worked. In fact, Sullivan often refers to him as the luckiest bastard."

Nice cop is long gone now. "Do you have any proof that this guy twisted his testimony?" He asks.

Tara sounds calm and collected. I'm sure she's damn good at her job too. "No. Sorry, dad."

"That's fine," he says, shaking his head. I can see the disappointment in his face. "I'll work with what I have. You and I are going to talk about this job of yours later tonight." He says before he hangs up.

30

LEVI

WITHIN THE HOUR, the ankle monitor is off and I'm ready to get the hell out of here, and not just because I'm glad to be off of house arrest. I just don't want to stay another moment under the same roof as my mom. I need a shower and to get rid of these clothes, but I don't even bother doing that. Officer Meija stayed at my request, since my dad texted me saying they got in early, and I guess decided to say to hell with quarantining since they were on the way to the apartment.

"Are you sure you don't want to come stay with me and the guys?" I ask Krissy as I stuff as many things as I can in a duffel bag. "Marcia said you can stay with her too, if you're more comfortable with that."

"No, it's okay. Marcia just got back from the hospital. She doesn't need extra guests, and my parents would disown me if they found out I was staying in a house full of male rockstars," she laughs. "I'll just stay until Riley's mom gets in town – whenever that is, and then I'll stay with her at the hotel."

She must see the heartbreak in my eyes when I look at her. "Riley will be okay," she assures me.

"Yep. And that is why I want to do what I told you. Please tell me you're going to help."

She smiles at me. "Yes. But I approve everything," she says. I figured that assuming the reporter gets me the footage, there should be videos of Riley dancing on the rooftop. In between that and videos Krissy has of them at recitals over the years, we should have enough to build her a portfolio to send in with her application for the school and for the scholarship.

"Are you still not going to tell me the story about the scholarship?" I ask her.

Krissy sighs. "She told her mom she got a scholarship so that her mom would spend her college money on the trip with her aunt. The trip was on her Aunt's bucket list."

I stop packing for a moment. "Wow," I say. Although I'm not at all surprised that Riley would do that.

"What is going on? Levi Jameson!" I hear mom's voice. "And why is there a dog in my apartment?"

"That is my cue to leave," I swing the duffel bag over my shoulder and grab the guitar, not worrying about what I'm leaving behind. I look back at Krissy. "Also, I'm bringing Wilson with me – at least until Riley's mom can take him back home or to the hotel. Whatever works. Just, please explain it to her why he's here and let me know when I should get him to you."

"Thank you," Krissy says to my surprise. "I think Riley will love to hear that you took care of him."

I get to the living room, with Krissy following from a distance. Officer Meija is standing by the door.

My dad and sister are both crouched down petting Wilson, while mom is standing, staring in my direction. High heels tapping on the floor as she waits for an explanation.

She yanks the mask off. "Why is there a cop in my house? What did you do now?"

"Nothing," I tell her, then I say hi to dad and Carly, who silently watch the interaction and stay out of it, like they always have.

"That is right. You never do anything," she snarls. "I just wish that was the case when it came to my student. She wouldn't be on a ventilator right now, destroying her career as minutes go by, if you had actually done nothing."

I flinch. We haven't had a good relationship during the past few years, but this is heartless and cruel. Even for her. And those words hit me. Hard. Not because of her saying it, but because in a way, she is right.

"Evelyn, that is enough!" My dad says, standing up.

"And where do you think you're going with that bag? You're on house arrest," she demands, looking at Officer Meija for reinforcement.

"He's free to go, ma'am," he says in a stern voice. And I can tell he's trying really hard to keep to himself.

"Who authorized this?" She practically growls at the cop. I shake my head, knowing she's three seconds away from asking to speak to his superiors, when he cocks his head to the side, and in a calm tone, he says, "It was authorized after we received confirmation that he was set up. Ma'am."

I can see the moment the blood drains from her face.

Officer Meija nods over toward the door. "Come on Wilson," I say, tapping on the side of my leg. He comes running. I grab his leash by the door, put it on and we follow Officer Meija out, without looking back.

31

TWO WEEKS LATER

LEVI

It's now been a week since Riley came off the ventilator and they turned off the drip so she would wake up from the medically induced coma. And it's been a long week of waiting for her to wake up, with no signs of any change. And it's been hell. Although, Wilson became a blessing in disguise. Krissy sent me a message on behalf on Riley's mom asking if I could keep him until she could take him home. So we keep each other company. He keeps me busy, but I can tell he's just as sad as I am.

Every single day, I've been begging for her to wake up with the promise that when she does, I'll stay out of her path so she can do what she's meant to.

In the meantime, Wilson and I get to see her almost every day.

I don't like to abuse my status as a rockstar, but when a nurse reached out to me saying that she was a huge fan of

Riley and me and thought that it would help Riley to hear my voice. My heart almost leapt out of my chest with hope. She said she could facilitate that during her shifts, I didn't think twice about saying, *yes, please!*

The moment I replied, I hoped and prayed this wasn't some con or some crazy person trying to just get me on the phone, but her social media profile checked out. Was it okay for her to do this without Riley's mom knowing? No clue. I learned a while back to not ask too many questions.

Today is the third day in a row this week that I get to talk to Riley. Only today, I got some good news for her.

"Ready?" Kelly, the angel nurse asks, smiling. "Hi Wilson," she says when he pops up on the screen, sitting next to me. He barks in response and she laughs. This has been our routine lately.

"Yep. Thanks again for this. I know you said to stop thanking you, but I can't."

She chuckles. "Well, I'm going to put my phone down and check on the patients nearby so you have some privacy."

"Thank you."

She flips the camera over, and it hits me every time. The tubes, the monitors… I would do anything to trade places with Riley right now.

"Hey, Sleeping Beauty," I say. "Got lots to tell you today. First," I say proudly. "Your admissions letter came in today. You got in, Riley." I pause. "No word on the scholarship yet, but Krissy said your Aunt Lilly left enough money for you that you won't have to worry about it. I know you'd rather have her here, Riley, and I know you're going to have a hard time using that money, but she was proud of you. She would've wanted you to do this." I look at her, hoping she'll open her eyes at any moment. When she doesn't, I sigh. "On to other things... My interview was featured yesterday. Marcia quit her job the moment she read it. I know that she quit through a text sent to my mom, and I'm sure she had a whole lot more to say." I smile, glad for having Marcia in my life. "But she's doing good, and me and the guys hired her to take care of our place in the city, even when we're not around. And I'm pretty sure my dad is about to ask mom for a divorce based on what Carly said. Fuck. I'm not supposed to be telling you depressing stuff."

I let out a breath. "I'm almost done with your song," I say and I put the phone on my dresser, grab the guitar and sing what I have so far.

I get to the part where I'm stuck, but this time, Wilson starts howling and I choke up, just wishing more than anything that she was awake. I lean my head down, petting his head.

"L-levi" I hear the sound of her croaky voice as the machines start to go off. Kelly rushes into the room, grabbing the phone. "I'll call you back," she says and she hangs up.

Minutes later, I get a message from her.

Kelly: She is awake!!!

I exhale and type a message back.

Me: Thank you. You'll never know how thankful I am for what you did for me.

I feel the weight of the world lifting off my shoulders, but I also know this means this is the last time I'll see her for a while. That was my promise. She lives. She wakes up. And I leave.

RILEY

ANOTHER WEEK LATER

"Who does this??" I say to Krissy as I pace back and forth in our hotel room. "Completely off the grid. No phone. Nothing. Until they're ready for their next tour. Next year?? Surely he has to practice with the guys before they have a show," I say.

I look at Wilson. Krissy told me that Levi took care of him while I was in the hospital, and then made reservations at a hotel that allows pets the moment he knew when I'd be released. And then... he left.

"He got the new manager to agree to do mostly the old sets during the first few shows – with one or two new songs. He said they'll just wing it," she laughs. "That new manager has a hell of alot of confidence in them," Krissy says, flipping the page on the magazine. "By the way, your mom is going to kill me if she knew I showed you this. You're not supposed to be stressed out. You barely just got out of the hospital."

"I'm not stressed. I'm mad. Ugh. Go on. Read the next question," I say and Krissy goes back to reading the feature on Levi's "Tell All" interview.

"You and Riley. What's the real story?"

I can practically see the smirk on his face after hearing the question.

"For me, it was love at first sight," Krissy stops to look for my reaction, and yeah, I'm frozen in place and considerably less mad. She smiles and goes back to it. "I heard a very smart person once say that the right people come into your life at the exact moment when you need them. Riley is it for me. In ways that she'll probably never know, she helped me find a part of myself that I had lost, or was losing..."

I sigh. Thinking about the time when Aunt Lilly told me that before.

"What does the future hold for you and Riley?"

"That is all up to her. She is insanely talented and focused, and right now, I'm sure she's out dancing somewhere. At least, I hope she is. It's what she'd dreamed of her whole life."

"So you are saying that you will wait for her while she lives her dream?"

Krissy looks from the magazine to me as I eagerly wait for her to go on.

"Yeah," Krissy reads, holding the magazine to her chest and smiling like it's the sweetest thing she ever heard.

"Idiot," I say.

Krissy laughs.

"He really believes in you," she says. "He created your portfolio, with my approval of course, and sent out the applications."

I gape. "He did?"

She nods.

"So what's next, Riley?" She asks me.

"You're getting really good at this," I tell her.

She shrugs. "I'm a natural."

"I still can't believe you're not going to school with me," I whine, although I am really happy that she's happy.

Krissy tilts her head. "But we still get to be roomies. Just a change in majors and school. I mean, someone has got to make sure that truthful journalism is happening here. Plus, the guys hired me as their social media genius, so I'm stuck going where they go," she smirks then grabs her phone, points it at me and asks again, "So, what is next, Riley Andrews?" She asks.

"A whole lot of waiting since someone decided to go off the grid," I roll my eyes at her.

"Can I upload it?" She asks. "On the off chance he sees it?"

"Yeah," I tell her.

Over the next few days, his fans go as far as setting up challenges to find Levi, and I cave. I get on social media, looking for clues. I watch the video of the famous kiss. I watch the stunning videos he created of me dancing so I could get into my dream school, and every video I see, every comment from his friends about him taking care of Wilson, the nurse's words about when he talked to me for hours while I wasn't even awake... everything makes me fall more and more in love with him.

As time goes by, I'm pretty sure it would be easier to find someone who is in witness protection. But thanks to

Aunt Lilly and Levi, I start classes at my dream school. Virtually at first, then in super small classes.

After a while, the challenges stop.

People move on.

Except for me.

I wait.

32

ONE YEAR LATER

LEVI

It's our first concert in over a year. Our opening show is in Manhattan, and I just got back to the city this afternoon. Our current manager is officially ready to kill me, but nothing new there... I guess he's now officially broken in. Tonight, I do what I usually do. I hide behind a flannel shirt, jeans, baseball cap, sunglasses, mask, and I disappear into the small crowd. The stage is pitch black – no lights at all – and the moment I start to hear the intro of the classical song that Riley loves morphing into the instrumental version of the one I wrote for her, I start to wonder what the fuck they are doing back there.

A few weeks ago, I mailed it to Bentley to get his opinion on the song. But that was it. It wasn't even finished. This song isn't even supposed to be in the set list for tonight, let alone for an opening act to play and sing it.

Fuck. No.

I stop to wonder if it is a tech issue, then I see the smoke begin to take over the stage, and I start to head in Xavier's direction. He sees me and shakes his head as Krissy makes her way to me, "Stay put, turn around, and watch," Xavier says into my earpiece. I do. I mean, I'm confused and slightly annoyed, but whatever. You'd think after spending a year in a cabin in the woods, alone, I would be all zen and shit. Nope.

The crowd starts to cheer. "Hey stranger," Krissy yells over the crowd.

I can't help but smile. I missed her too. "Nice hair," I say, talking about her now, pink highlights. She shrugs, leaning into me. "It was time for a change."

I feel like my heart is about to leap out of my chest as I nervously ask my next question.

"Is she coming?" I made sure Bentley gave Krissy back-stage passes for Riley. I hold my breath as she glares at me. "One year, man," she says into my ear. "Did you really think she was gonna wait around for that long?"

I look down, feeling crushed. Shit. I guess she's right. I shake my head, then I feel Krissy bump into my shoulder. I look at her, glad that the sunglasses are hiding my reaction. She nods over toward the stage.

The first thing I see through the smoke is a pair of bright sparkly red ballet slippers. I follow it up, recognizing every curve, until my eyes land on hers. She's wearing a black leotard, black tutu, hair in a bun, and she's holding one of my guitars like it's a prop. Then she reaches for her hair, shakes her head from side to side, long locks falling over her shoulders. She adjusts the guitar, holding it just right. And holy fuck. That is hot.

Behind the stupid mask, there's a huge smile on my face. And then she starts to strum the chords, while standing in *'releve'* position. Don't ask me how the fuck I know that. And she looks RIGHT. AT. ME.

I just stand here, gaping.

Bentley takes the mic and starts to sing the song I wrote for her. He gets through two lines, the crowd is getting into it, and then he stops. Riley continues playing the guitar as if she isn't surprised at all that he stopped. She is in her zone like she does with dancing. *'When did she learn to play?'* I wonder. Then Bentley says into the mic, "Sorry, everyone. This feels wrong. Get your ass up here Levi O'Connor and sing to your girl."

The crowd goes crazy, and they look around, following Riley's gaze on me.

"Run," Xavier yells into my earpiece as people around start to look at me.

I jog toward Xavier, ditching the flannel shirt on the way. When I get to him, I get rid of the sunglasses and the hat, and I don't even go backstage. I just climb up the stage through the front, ditch the mask, and go straight to Riley.

She stops playing when I get close enough and in spite of the thousands of people spread out around here, for the moment, there is complete silence.

"May I?" I reach for the guitar.

She hands it to me and my fingers brush against hers and the chemistry is almost electrifying.

She's expecting me to play, instead, I hand it to Bentley. Looking into her eyes, I close the distance between us, putting my hand on the small of her back and pulling her toward me.

I give her a crooked smile.

"Are you about done making me wait?" She asks.

I smile at her. "I thought I was the one waiting," I say against her lips, before I kiss her. I feel her hands through my hair, and this kiss is different. She's all in. Just like I am.

The crowd is still cheering when she pulls away to catch her breath.

"So, how does the song end?" She whispers against my lips. I notice the silence surrounding us as if everyone else is waiting on that answer too, and without looking away from her, I extend my hand for Bentley to give me the guitar. I lace my fingers through hers and nod over for Bentley to take over, hoping we have an actual opening act. Preferably a long one.

"What are we doing?" Riley asks as I lead her backstage.

I keep walking, with her by my side. I glance at her and give her a crooked smile, "This song is just for you," I tell her. "Someone taught me they don't have to have every piece of my life. Not anymore."

"Someone, huh?" She chuckles.

We get to the back and I stop walking. I face her and reach for a lock of her hair, tucking it behind her ear, as I take her in. She looks just as beautiful as she did a year ago, but so much more confident… happier. And a part of me can't believe how lucky I am that she waited.

"Does that someone get to have every piece of you?" She asks, and I smirk and raise an eyebrow while my arms pull her in as close as possible to me. She shakes her head and looks away, and I'm thrilled I still get to make her blush like this.

I brush a finger against her chin, tilting her head up. "You get every piece. And more." She wraps her arms around my neck and pulls me in for a passionate kiss. I'm left breathless for a moment and hold her tight as I whisper in her ear, "And that, is how the song ends."

THE END

LIFE INTERRUPTED – RILEY'S SONG

SHINING LIGHT

So long ago, I reached for the stars
it's all I've ever known, to play a part
I gave my all to the only thing I've known
but there's an emptiness in my heart

I thought I was just broken
destined to fake the smile
leave it all unspoken
mind running mile after mile

(But You)
You opened my eyes
showed me how to live
You took my hand
told me there's much more to give
I was a fool for not seeing
what was right in front of me
with you
is where I'm supposed to be

How many times you've talked me back from the edge
can we start over, begin again
I swear this until my last breath
give me a chance, I'll love you til the end

At the end of the day
you're the only one on my mind
knowing just what to say
a shining light to guide my way

ABOUT DANIELE LANZAROTTA

Daniele Lanzarotta is the author of young adult and new adult paranormal/fantasy/contemporary novels, including *The Sinners Series, Academy of the Fallen Series, Life Interrupted* and more.

Daniele is the CEO & Founder of Elysian Nightfall Studios – audio & video post-production, brand development and screenwriting services company. She is also the A/V Director at The Audio Flow, and a Board Member with Youth in the Booth.

Writing and working with audiobooks and TV/Film is her passion. She has undergraduate studies in Digital Cinematography, a MBA with focus in marketing - specializing in brand development, and Certification in Media Communications. In addition to having worked on post-production for several audiobooks in diverse genres, she has also worked on Virginia based short films as the 2nd Assistant Director and Still Photographer.

She enjoys watching hockey, playing Rock Band/Guitar Hero, traveling, and spending time with her husband, two daughters, and the family dog.

ALSO BY DANIELE LANZAROTTA

Academy of the Fallen Series – YA

Wide Awake

Nephilim

Sins of the Fallen

Forsaken

Sudden Hope Novels – YA

Sudden Hope

Catch Me If I Fall

Imprinted Souls Series – YA

Imprinted Souls

Bloodlust

Divine Ashes

Blood Bound

Shattered Souls

Imprinted Souls Series Spin-off - YA

Venom

Havenwood Falls (Shared World Series)

Avenoir – YA

Blurred Lines –YA

Lost Souls – A Series of Short Horror Stories - YA

Lost Souls Vol 1

Lost Souls Vol 2

A Mermaid's Curse Trilogy – Adult

Insatiable

Fated

Unbreakable

The Sinner's Series – Adult

Sinners

Lust

Individual Titles

The Right Kind of Wrong – Adult

www.ingramcontent.com/pod-product-compliance
Lightning Source LLC
Chambersburg PA
CBHW060548310726
48982CB00008B/1052/J

* 9 7 8 1 0 8 7 8 7 8 9 2 8 *